THE LAKE WOBEGON VIRUS

THE LAKE WOBEGON VIRUS

A NOVEL

GARRISON KEILLOR

ARCADE PUBLISHING • NEW YORK

First Edition

This is a work of fiction. Names, places, characters, and incidents are either the products of the author's imagination or are used fictitiously.

Arcade Publishing books may be purchased in bulk at special discounts for sales promotion, corporate gifts, fund-raising, or educational purposes. Special editions can also be created to specifications. For details, contact the Special Sales Department, Arcade Publishing, 307 West 36th Street, 11th Floor, New York, NY 10018 or arcade@skyhorsepublishing.com.

Arcade Publishing® is a registered trademark of Skyhorse Publishing, Inc.®, a Delaware corporation.

Visit our website at www.arcadepub.com.
Visit the author's site at garrisonkeillor.com.

10 9 8 7 6 5 4 3 2 1

Library of Congress Cataloging-in-Publication Data is available on file.
Library of Congress Control Number: 2020941333

Cover design by Brian Peterson
Cover illustration: Rodica Prato

ISBN: 978-1-951627-67-6
Ebook ISBN: 978-1-951627-69-0

Printed in the United States of America

THE LAKE WOBEGON VIRUS

1

FEBRUARY 16, 6:30 A.M.

Well, it has been a quiet year in Lake Wobegon except for the heat wave in February and then that weird epidemic of what's called "episodic loss of inhibition" and sensible Germans and Norwegians pouring out inappropriate feelings, spilling crazy secrets, hallucinating about some conspiracy or other, acting out—Darlene baring her breasts at the Chatterbox Cafe— Dorothy stopped her in time, but still—our beloved Darlene, the last of the old-time waitresses who called their clients "Sweetheart," at 55 opening her blouse!—and Pastor Liz making a fool of herself in a Sunday sermon. And Clint coming out as an atheist and Father Wilmer caught in carnal thoughts, the postmaster Mr. Bauser observed while on duty singing, "*The State Department and Internal Revenue are promoting a One World point of view. Obama was a Kenyan man, took the oath of office on a Koran. Don't be brainwashed by the press, they're promoting godlessness,*" and then saw Myrtle waiting to buy stamps. She said, "Are you supposed to be singing songs on the job?" She went out and told Clarence Bunsen, and Clarence came and talked to him, and Mr. Bauser denied all. And from then on, he returned Myrtle's letters to her, marked "Address Illegible," though she went to school back when good penmanship was taught and hers was A+. And somebody—guess who?—put her name on the mailing list of the American Free Love Party. It was ugly. When I came to town in March, people said, "I hope you aren't going to write about this," which of course aroused my curiosity since I had no idea what they meant and so I stuck around to find out.

That same day, Arlen Hoerschgen walked up to the check-out desk at the library, and Grace, gentle Grace, ever-patient Grace, looked at the book of limericks he wanted to check out and said, "When in hell are you going to grow up?" And she quoted a dozen dirty limericks at him, including:

> There was a young girl of Eau Claire
> Who was graceful and so debonaire,
> But she did not pee
> Like a girl, downwardly,
> But could aim up high in the air.

and others even worse and said, "I tell you, the apple doesn't fall far from the tree. I remember your ne'er-do-well uncle going around town tanked up on sloe gin and singing filthy songs in broad daylight like the one about the shepherd and the magpie, and his poor children were so ashamed of him they all went off and became Seventh-day Adventists." And she stamped the due date on it and handed it to him, and he felt sort of sheepish and returned with it 20 minutes later to apologize, and she had no memory of it whatsoever. "Where'd this come from?" she said. "Read whatever you like." Loss of inhibition followed by memory loss.

Mrs. Torgerson entered a national talent contest performing "Bridge Over Troubled Water" on Audubon bird whistles, all six and one-half minutes of it, and Bob took off on a long road trip to visit relatives in Oregon and Washington while she rehearsed. Neighbors said the artistry was incredible, sometimes involving three or four whistles at once, but the effect of the whole was to make you reach for your gun.

It was craziness, and it set neighbor against neighbor, Norwegian against German, a town that prided itself on sobriety and responsibility and modest behavior, and meanwhile, looming on the horizon was the very real threat of a Keep America Truckin' Museum and Motorway in the planning stages south of town, featuring a mile oval for racing 18-wheelers—farmland was already being bought up for the thing—annual attendance estimated to be 2.2 million visitors, many with huge tattoos and carrying six-guns and six-packs, and rumor had it there'd be a six-lane freeway and a couple of high-rise hotels on the outskirts of town and maybe a casino. An absolute nightmare. The "Little Town That Time Forgot" suddenly becoming the little town that Misfortune fell in love with, where all the women are horrified, the men are bewildered, and the children are amused at the distress of their elders.

Dorothy of the Chatterbox said, "It's been like a horror novel but with actual people, you wouldn't want to read it but you are living it." In the midst of a town council meeting, Mayor Eloise Krebsbach jumped up, threw her gavel out the window not noticing it was closed, and said, "This town has gone to the dogs and as far as I'm concerned, they can have it." She took a job as a nail salon hostess in St. Paul and was replaced by Alice Dobbs, a newcomer to town (1995), who feels that problems have solutions and if we commit ourselves to the common good, we can find our way out of the woods.

Lenny, a Wobegon girl who left home to become an epidemiologist, came home during a bitter divorce and diagnosed the problem, and Alice, over fierce opposition, brought in a municipal therapist though people here don't do therapy or discuss unpleasant feelings. If someone asks, "How are you?" you say, Fine. And that's good enough. It could be worse. You go into therapy and you are apt to get engrossed in yourself and neglect your children and they turn out fragile and moody and take up songwriting or conceptual baking. But the therapist, Ashley, turned out to be a very nice person, mannerly, soft-spoken, once you got to know her. And in the midst of it all, I arrived to work on a sainthood project and thought about writing this book instead, but now I'm getting ahead of myself.

Where to begin?

It began on February 16th at about 6:30 a.m. in the Chatterbox Cafe when the old waitress Darlene leaned down and said to Daryl Tollerud, "You disgust me, and you know why? Because you never make eye contact, there's never a 'Good morning' or 'How are you, Darlene?'—you sit there waiting for the world to do your bidding and bring your bacon and eggs, and when I bring it, you stare at my boobs. It's like you never saw a woman before. Twenty years you've been staring at them. Well, here they are—" And she tore open her shirt and there they were for a split second until Dorothy grabbed her, and Darlene picked up the plate and smooshed it in his face as fried egg yolk ran down his shirt along with hash browns and bacon, and she turned and stalked away. People around him pretended nothing had happened, which Lake Wobegon people are adept at doing. They could ignore an anvil falling out of a tree so long as it didn't fall on them.

Dorothy cleaned him up and apologized, and Daryl felt bad about what she said, realizing there was some truth to it. It went back to when he was 16 and attended a carnival sideshow at the county fair and saw a contortionist named Maria who folded herself up to fit inside a breadbox and then handed her brassiere up to the ringmaster, and if you liked you could pay a quarter to go and look into the breadbox and Daryl did, and there she was, all folded up, her arms wrapped around her chest, and ever since then Daryl has felt a thrill at the sight of a woman with folded arms.

Minutes later, Darlene emerged from the ladies' room as if nothing had happened, and when Dorothy said, "What's wrong with you?" Darlene had no idea what she meant. "You spilled all down the front of your shirt," she said to Daryl. "Don't eat so fast." Somebody told her she had bared her bosom. She said, "Good God, who do you take me for?" Daryl is a forgiving soul—he had four teenage children living under his roof at one time, one of them a Goth and a shoplifter, another a drummer—and also he felt he was responsible for what happened, a common reaction among Lutherans.

He finished his breakfast and went home and heard a voice from the bedroom—"Is that you?"—and of course it was him, who else would she imagine it might be? He felt a twinge of jealousy, and then there she was, half in her lingerie and half out, approaching him in a meaningful way, and said, "I was waiting for you." His old Marilyn, mother of his five children, in the mood for love at eight thirty in the morning, will wonders never cease? She had been the most beautiful woman in town, and when she was young and went dancing at the Moonlight Bay Supper Club, men fought in the parking lot for the right to dance with her. Men cursing, fists on bone, she was so lovely, and that's how she came to marry Daryl. All the fighting men were in a rage and she walked away with a pacifist.

It was an historic week for her and Daryl. They had rid themselves of a Chihuahua named Mitzi who was bought over Daryl's objections, he being an old farmboy brought up to believe dogs live outdoors so they can run off interlopers and in payment for this service, we feed them. A Chihuahua serves no purpose except to share its anxieties. One day in February, the dog, on a toilet run, encountered a skunk. The dog had never imagined such a thing as a skunk existing—had no idea what the purpose of one would be—and the skunk unloaded, and Daryl grabbed the .22 and ran out and met the skunk, who still had some left in him, and Daryl didn't even get off a shot. Mitzi had a nervous breakdown and Daryl showered for an hour and still had some skunk in his hair, so Marilyn clipped his head clean and Mitzi went off to live with cousin Janice in the city. Daryl slept in the guest room for a week and now, evidently, was attractive again.

She kissed him and unbuckled his belt and placed his hand on her bosom, and he stepped out of his shoes and his masculinity hung loose like a graduation tassel. He was spectacularly impotent. She tried to get its attention, but it was thinking of other things. After years of embarrassing involuntary erections in public—walking around with a ball-peen hammer in his pants—Darlene's attack on him had removed the lead from his pencil. His billiard cue had turned into a curtain sash.

And two days later, an anonymous person left a gift for Darlene: a new bra made of molded plastic with a combination lock on the strap. It was a joke, but Darlene took it badly, and days later she packed up and left town without a word and the loss was felt immediately.

Some people are irreplaceable, and in a small town we know who they are. Darlene is a font of information about local history and who is married to whom and where their kids wound up and what they do. For example, David and Judy Ingqvist, the former pastor and his wife—retired, Napa Valley, hikers and bikers, switched to Unitarian, daughter Brenda is a professional pet grief therapist, author of *Mourning Your Cat,* conducts pet grief seminars and several annual pet grief cruises to the Caribbean. Nobody but Darlene can give you this level of detail.

She also rules over the potluck suppers in town, receives the offerings and arranges them on the serving tables, and when she is away, the number of store-bought dishes quadruples—big tubs of yellowish potato salad rather than homemade, factory-made lasagna. With Darlene as gatekeeper, people are inspired to make an effort, and with her gone, there is a great slacking-off, and you don't want that in a small town. What if your firemen and EMTs and teachers start to slack off? What if your neighbors see your window wide open in the pouring rain and think, "Oh what the hell. Not my problem."

And beyond that, she's from a previous era when waitresses might call you "Darling" or "Sweetheart" or "Sugar," and if she knows you well, you'd be "Honeybunch" or "Sweetykins" or "Precious." Maybe she'd ask what you want and you'd say, "The usual," and she'd pinch the flab under your chin and say, "Maybe we've been having too much of the usual, darling." With her gone, nobody would ever be "Precious" again. She was missed by all the old men whose wives no longer sweet-talk them. Once, Duane Bunsen, home from his IT job in a Minneapolis bank, came back for a weekend and was Honeybunched by Darlene and went back to Minneapolis and called his office manager "Sweetheart" and was spoken to sharply. But in this town, Sweet-hearting and Preciousing between adults who've known each other since childhood is considered a comfort. And you, beloved reader, should take my word for it. I'm not kidding, Pumpkin.

It was a time of strange phenomena. Daryl and David Darwin, the one-time bullies of the town who loved fistfights more than life itself, now approaching 80, their hands having been busted so many times they cannot shuffle a deck of cards or handle a wrench—they stood in Wally's Sidetrack Tap among the cribbage game, the basketball on TV, the pinball machine dinging, both of them tipsy on peach brandy, and they broke into "Love's Old Sweet Song," a favorite of their mother's, sang it in sweet two-part harmony like Don and Phil Everly. The pinball stopped, the TV sound was turned down. Two rotten sinners and hell-raisers, but something had moved them and they sang from the depths of their blackened hearts, "*Tho' the heart be weary, sad the day and long, still to us at twilight comes love's old song, comes love's old sweet song.*"

Wally said, "That was beautiful, boys," and then he sneezed so hard he blew his cigar across the room, shedding sparks like a comet, and he threw out his sacroiliac. He looked for the cigar and found it under a radiator, and there beside it was a letter postmarked 2017, addressed to Daryl Darwin when he was in jail for malicious cruelty, written by his mother, Millie, on her deathbed and delivered three years late, which said, "Darling Daryl, I love you dearly and though you have hurt me deeply, I forgive you, and as I prepare to leave this world, I want you to know that I see the good in you and am proud to be your mom." Nobody ever had said good things about Daryl Darwin and here he'd been forgiven from beyond the grave, and he and David sang their mother's favorite song, tears running down their cheeks, and men in the bar who bore scars inflicted by the Darwins wept along with them.

The same day Darlene got the bra, the Men's Fellowship, a group of 30 or so who used to be the Men's Prayer Fellowship but gradually devolved into a social club, met for lunch at the Legion hall. It was always old man Bunsen who had prayed, Clarence and Clint's dad, Oscar, and when dementia struck, he prayed in Norwegian, which was so majestic men wept to hear it, though they couldn't understand a word, and when he died, few ventured to pray a real prayer, knowing the result would be inferior. Oscar was widely revered. On the day he died, at age 82, though out of his mind, he came to town and enjoyed a hearty lunch, had a beer at the Sidetrack, won three bucks at cribbage, told three jokes well, danced to "The Too Fat Polka" with Wally's wife, who was tending bar, walked three miles home, lay down for a nap and never awoke.

9

The Fellowship sat down to chicken chow mein and coleslaw at two long tables, and everyone murmured, "God is great and God is good, and we thank Him for the food. By His hand, we must be fed. Give us, Lord, our daily bread." And then Clint Bunsen stood up as they started to dig in and said, "I have to say that the idea that there is a daddy in the sky who is arranging our lives and doing favors in exchange for our admiration is an old hoax, and everybody knows it deep down in your hearts and doesn't dare say it. If he is a god of goodness and he doesn't use his power to wipe out evil, then he isn't omnipotent and there's no reason to worship him. God is a wrong turn we took back in antiquity, and it is responsible for more hatred and warfare and cruelty than anything else, and yet our grandfathers handed it to our fathers and they gave it to us, and I say, No, thank you. Wake up, live your life, be glad for what you have, and don't let delusions of godliness blind you to the beauty of nature." And he sat down and dug into his chicken chow mein. And Roger asked Clarence if Clint was okay, and he said, "He was an hour ago."

Conversation was muted after that and stuck mainly to the weather, the long-term forecasts. It was Lent, after all, and Lutheran men sign a Lenten pledge to observe 10 hours of silence a week, which for some of them would be a normal day. Anyway, they didn't talk about atheism.

When Clarence caught up with him later, Clint, unlike Darlene, did not deny having said what he said. He said he'd heard a TED Talk by a woman who said that deism is destructive to our ability to empathize, that it dehumanizes us, and he'd been listening to her podcast, so some of her thoughts were running through his head and something moved him to speak them aloud, so he did, and he didn't feel embarrassed, quite the contrary. His granddaughters had been encouraged to express themselves freely, and now they are all over the map ideologically, anarcho-humanist, animal activist, post-behavioral feminism, witchcraft, and he feels okay about stepping out of the Comfy Grampa role and staking out some ground for himself.

Clarence pointed out the obvious—that their Ford dealership, Bunsen Motors, is traditionally patronized by Lutherans, rather than the Catholic Krebsbach Chev, and so it might be prudent to keep any atheist thoughts to himself lest Ford owners feel a divine calling to buy Chevs instead. Perhaps an apology to the Men's Fellowship would be in order. Clint declined to apologize. "I feel like I've been apologizing all my life and that's enough." He said it felt good to say his piece, and it made people sit up and think, and how can you be opposed to thoughtfulness?

"There is truth in what you say, I'm sure, but we have a business to think of," said Clarence.

"Ha! A dying business. You and I are old, and none of our kids are interested in selling cars or working on them, believe me, I've asked. Duane's happy in Minneapolis, Harry does comic books, Donna's in real estate, Barbara Ann runs her husband Bill and elects Democrats. And what fool is going to buy a small-town Ford dealership that runs 85 percent on personal loyalty? New owner comes in, and suddenly all the Lutherans are free to shop around and buy Japanese. There's a big Ford dealership just down the road that undersells us by 10 to 15 percent. You know it and I know it. You're looking at retirement, Bubs. Another year or two and you can stop combing the hair over your bald spot and get yourself a bigger color TV."

"Okay, okay," Clarence said. "Think what you like, but don't feel you have to share it with the world, okay? Spare me the headache. No need to go around desecrating things." And Clint nodded and slid back under the car—a quart of peanut butter had melted into the heater and needed to be vacuumed and squeegeed out—reason enough, Clarence thought, to lose faith in God temporarily. He noticed on the workbench a white lily and a chocolate-covered doughnut and a Post-it note, "You're my hero. I love you." In Irene's handwriting. He'd been counting on Irene's help. No such luck.

Clint had had his doubts about Christianity for years, having been the Samaritan who goes out on emergency calls with the wrecker to rescue Christians with car problems. Hundreds of times he had stood beside a motorist staring helplessly at his engine and taking the Lord's name in vain and Clint reached down and flicked something, and the car leaped to life, and the Christian hated him for fixing it so quickly (couldn't he have pretended to be confused and said, "Boy, I dunno, this is a toughie," but no, he just reached down and bingo). So the Christian hands him a ten, and Clint says, "No, no, my pleasure," and he smiles and pats the Christian's arm, and walks away, and it's the pat on the arm that pisses the Christian off, the patronizing pat of the big hero of the highway, and you're the goat. No, Clint had helped many a stranded Christian and heard his teeth grinding as he walked away.

Now he expected Pastor Liz to come and have a word with him about faith and offer him some helpful pamphlets to read, and he planned to tell her, "I decided it's time to face the darkness and not be afraid," and two days later Pastor Liz went over the cliff.

The next Sunday morning, she seemed distracted, she didn't join in the opening hymn, she stood up to give the sermon. The rule about sermons is: they should have a clear beginning and a strong end, and the two should be as close together as possible. Liz is dyslexic, so she tries to memorize the sermon, but she carries blank paper with her because Lutherans get nervous if the pastor in the pulpit has no text, they worry that she'll go on at length and the pot roast will burn in the oven.

This sermon got away from her, and it went on for almost an hour. It started out on the verse in Colossians about Christ interceding for us at the right hand of the throne of God, and the word "throne" flipped a switch, and she told about the time she flew to Boston and used the toilet on the plane, not noticing the warning sign "Do Not Flush While Seated on Toilet," because she was sitting on the toilet at the time, and she flushed and felt a powerful force gripping her butt like a python seizing a rat, and she couldn't pry herself loose. The flight attendant was tapping on the door and asking, "Are you all right?" and Pastor Liz didn't know how to answer that question. She was basically all right in that she had faith in God's unceasing love, but on the other hand, she was being swallowed by a toilet. The flight attendant tried to break the seal by inserting his hand between the toilet seat and her left cheek. But she was still stuck, and the plane had to make an emergency landing in Cleveland, and the ground crew cut the toilet free with an acetylene torch and lifted her out, the seat still stuck to her, and carried her through the terminal, toilet seat attached, and someone took a picture and it appeared on Instagram, Liz looking like a Parker House roll on a plate, with arms and legs. This picture made its way to the bishop, and so Liz, who'd been marked for a coveted assignment at prestigious Central Lutheran in Minneapolis, got shunted off to Lake Wobegon. Minneapolis Lutherans didn't want a pastor whose buttocks had gone viral online. One wrong flush, and though she'd been valedictorian at St. Olaf, she was sent to the sticks. The mention of St. Olaf then reminded her of the boy named Adam who took her virginity, but she had to beg him to do it, he didn't do it of his own volition, and then she talked about her cat, Muffin, who had a kidney infection, and then she went on a tirade against the church demoting the Holy Spirit, who is the feminine member of the Trinity—the congregation sat in shock and three people walked out, and then the organist, Tibby Marklund, who'd been working a crossword puzzle, planted her left foot on a pedal and there was a throbbing bass note like an ailing hippopotamus, and two altos burst out in horrible whinnying laughter, and Liz left and there was no Communion.

Lutherans are not amused by stream-of-consciousness sermons. Some people said, "Oh, she was only sharing her humanity," but phone calls were made by the elders, and on Monday morning Lutheran HQ sent a psychologist to talk to Liz, who had no memory of the sermon though she admitted the toilet-seat story was true, and the psychologist asked her if she had had a mental lapse of this sort previously, and Liz looked him in the eye and said, "I don't care for your tone of voice. I am a minister of the Gospel, I am not here for you to patronize. Go be snotty to somebody else." The next day she left quietly on an extended leave of absence with her sister Lil, who'd come all the way from Grand Forks to collect her. The cat was given to the Tolleruds, and that evening Daryl dosed it with a tranquilizer crushed in whipped cream, and Muffin went to the Great Lap in the Sky.

Lake Wobegon had never had a genuine clerical scandal before, and it made the most of this one, especially the Catholics did. They went out of their way to accost their Lutheran friends and express sympathy in a way that made you want to give them a good swift kick in the shins. Their sympathy was insufferable.

Myrtle Krebsbach said to Florence Tollefson, "I can't imagine what you people are going through right now. This must be terribly painful. She seemed like such a nice person."

Florence said, "Mind your own business for once."

"To sit there Sunday morning and listen to your own minister talk about getting stuck on a toilet seat and then losing her virginity to somebody who didn't even like her. In church. I can't imagine what it must've been like."

Florence's gaze drilled right into her. "Well, I'm glad we've given you all something to gossip about. Feast on it. Your turn will come, I promise."

"If there's anything I can do to help, I hope you'll let me know."

"You could start by losing 40 pounds and using less eye shadow. You're 80 years old, for God's sake."

"I'm only expressing my sympathy. I'm sorry this is so painful for you."

Florence said, "Well, you can take your sympathy and put it where the sun don't shine."

There was great delight in the Sidetrack Tap, of course, a place where decorum is not a fixed standard. Men took a toilet seat off the wall and passed it around, and Clint Bunsen, on his second rum and Coke, hung the seat around his neck and sang:

I used to work in Chicago
In a big department store.
I used to work in Chicago—
I did but I don't anymore.
A lady came in for a girdle.
I asked her what kind she wore.
"Rubber," she said, and rub her I did,
And I don't work there anymore.

And Mr. Bauer recited: "*There was a young pastor named Liz who sat on the toilet to whiz. She flushed and it stuck on her butt. WTF. And that's what her ass meant and is.*"

Clint split a gut, and then they did "Waltz Me Around Again, Willie" and "Roll Me Over in the Clover" and the dirty version of "Red Wing," and they told limericks about the young man from Antietam and the young lady of Buckingham. The Sidetrack Tap is not the American Academy of Arts and Letters, and it has its own rules. Of course, if Pope Francis walked in or Michelle Obama, people would behave accordingly, but meanwhile, it is what it is, and the old patrons took some pleasure in the chagrin of Lutherans at the Liz episode.

And so the town headed into March, the month God created to show people who don't drink what a hangover is like.

The Lutheran bishop sent a pale seminarian named Phipps to replace Liz. He was pleasant enough but had a terrible habit of strolling into the congregation during his sermon, approaching people, putting his hand on your shoulder, preaching face-to-face, which terrified people. What if he grabbed you suddenly and hollered, "Heal!"—what would you do? Lutherans are not Pentecostals, they're not looking for out-of-the-body experiences. So Phipps was sent back to the factory, and a young woman named Faith arrived who was Episcopalian as you could see from the rather ornate sash around her neck, like a sidecloth from your grandma's buffet, and good God, the way she genuflected with a deep curtsy—can't you cross yourself without making it into a ballet move? She did the Good Friday reading of Christ on the cross, and when she read, "My God, my God, why hast thou forsaken me?" it sounded like she was having an episode. And the Easter reading and the angel saying, "DO NOT BE ALARMED"—it was alarming. This is church, not *Masterpiece Theatre*. She was sent back.

Meanwhile, the inappropriate incidents went on. Margie Krebsbach sat down in the Bon Ton to have her hair done and started talking French to Charlotte. French! She spoke a whole slew of it. Charlotte remembers enough French from high school to recognize it as something of a communistic nature with the words *"Allons! Allons! Mes camarades!"* Then Margie closed her eyes and leaned back, and Charlotte did the usual and no more was said. Weird. It was Arlene Bunsen who read an article about inappropriate outbursts as a symptom of food poisoning, and she took it to Dr. DeHaven, who was busy with a man whose urinary tract was on the fritz, so she left the article for him and he wrote her a note before he went home for his nap. She had to find his old nurse Eleanor, who is the only person in town, including Dr. DeHaven, who can read his handwriting. He said, "I'm sorry, but I've got my hands full with people who actually need help. Your people are just competing for attention." Dr. DeHaven was 78 and had hinted at retirement years before but was offended that nobody tried to talk him out of it, and so he stayed on. He was a good man, but his general motto was "Let's wait and see," which doesn't always lead to good results. He was easily bored by people's complaints and often changed the subject to his own adventures as a hunter and fisherman and told one story after another until the appointment was up and thanked the patient and saw him or her to the door.

The Lutheran church was pastorless, so the bishop sent Rev. Anderson, a retiree, a pastor from the pasture, 82, who often neglected to wear his hearing aids and seemed quite content to be deaf. According to Lucille, who cleaned the parsonage as well as the church, he missed the toilet when he peed, and he took two-hour naps, sometimes two in succession. It was discovered after three weeks that his sermons came word-for-word from *Homily Helper,* a collection of 520 sermon outlines that he read as sermons, about three minutes in length. To Lutherans, those are known as "chalk talks," and they're meant for children. The man was shirking his duty.

Lutherans are dutiful people. Many Lutheran couples, after their wedding and the supper in the church basement, have stuck around to help with the dishes and cleaning up, even though their families tell them, "You go now. We're fine. It's your honeymoon, for heaven's sake," but the couple insists, "No, we don't want to leave you with the mess. As soon as we sweep up and clean off the tables, we'll be out of here." Elderly Lutherans have gone in the hospital and wished the pastor would come visit them but refused to let anyone tell him. They would rather die than be a problem, and often they do. But a three-minute sermon is an insult. So Clarence and Roger and Grace and Dorothy drove down to the Minneapolis Lutheran synod headquarters and arrived a few minutes before the 5 p.m. closing time, and the front door was locked, so Roger got out a lug wrench and banged on the glass until a bishop appeared, and they marched in without a word of apology, unusual for Lutherans, and told the bishop that Pastor Anderson was a disgrace to the vestments, and he was drummed out, and the next day Liz came back, good old Liz. She'd been accepted as an intern at an organic hydroponic herb farm owned by Ben, who was auditioning to be her boyfriend, but when the bishop called her, she felt a tug at her heartstrings, and besides, Ben—a Republican who believed that a Deep State of undercover Harvard liberals was running Washington—required more remedial work than she cared to invest in him, so she accepted her old job back and the next Sunday there she was, and as she came down the aisle, the congregation applauded. Highly unusual in a Lutheran church. Historic, even. But they'd seen the alternatives and compared to arrogance and sloth, a bare butt looked not so bad.

Wobegon is a town of nice people except for a few cranks who serve to show how nice everyone else is. Self-effacing people. Bare butts are not what Wobegon is about, not at all, and yet—once Lutherans had seen the grabby guy and the thespian and the slacker, they welcomed Liz back joyfully and forgivingly. It's good for a pastor to experience public shame and be forgiven. You practice on the pastor, and maybe someday you'll be capable of forgiving yourself.

2

HELL-RAISING MAN

While pastors came and went and people spoke out of turn and the Darwins wept for their mother, Roger Hedlund, the county assessor, took note of a whole series of farm sales—the Dickmeier, Tingvold, Halvorson, Kreuger, Pfleiderscheidt, and Schroeder farms, a considerable piece of real estate, sold to Dixon Holding in Nashville, and it troubled him though he was in the middle of a heated conversation with Mrs. Tollefson who was incensed at her tax bill. She said, "You, sir, are dumber than a boxful of hammers if you think my taxes went up by 40 percent in one year. If you were any slower, you'd be in reverse. Look at this. Look at it." And when he bent down to read the bill closely, she said, "Your toupee looks like a cat that a truck ran over," and gave it a yank, but it was his own hair, not a toupee, and she said, "Who did your hair? The undertaker?" And in the heat of the moment, he forgot about the farm sales until the subject came up in a planning commission meeting a week later, and a couple dozen citizens showed up to protest the Dickmeier sale, arguing that the World's Largest Pile of Burlap Bags, which the

Dickmeiers had built up over the years, which had gotten Lake Wobegon into the Guinness Book of World Records, should be protected as other noted sites such as the World's Largest Ball of Twine in a nearby town had been.

The Dickmeiers had begun building the Largest Pile in August 1965, out of thanksgiving for having survived the great tornado that struck to the north and west. A sunny day in Lake Wobegon, but debris was carried by high-altitude winds and out of a clear blue sky a barn door came flying in, whirling like a top, and a 1957 Chevrolet picked up from behind Helen's Hi-Top Lounge in Fergus Falls, which fell to earth missing the Dickmeiers' house, with nine children in it, by inches, judging by the fact that the TV antenna from the roof was found impaled in the car's left rear tire. The garden where the car hit was where the Largest Pile was begun. It incorporated a wooden crate that had contained 24 bowling balls and lifted off from the Breckenridge train depot in the twister, eventually splitting open and raining bowling balls on the town, one of which bounced on the loading dock behind Ralph's Grocery, flew a hundred feet in the air, and landed in the cemetery on the Dickmeier plot—a message from Above not to be ignored. The memorial Pile was raised, but of course, with time dedication flagged, and none of the Dickmeier children took an interest, and the grandchildren regarded it as a freakish absurdity, and so the land was sold.

Unfortunately, the Largest Pile had got onto the Internet as a source of phlogiston, a gaseous element believed to relieve kidney stones, and so vanloads of people suffering from painful urination made a pilgrimage to the Dickmeiers, which persuaded them to put up a fence and charge admission. The neighbors complained that many of the pilgrims, on their way home, stopped to relieve themselves in the ditches and woods. So the sheriff blocked the road, allowing access to residents only. He was sued by the Dickmeiers, and the case went all the way to the U.S. Supreme Court, which ruled, in *World's Largest Pile v. Sheriff Burnquist*, that a presumed purpose of public urination does not justify restriction of the freedom of movement, and the day the ruling came down, the freedom to pee was celebrated by hundreds in the Supreme Court plaza. People opposed to the sale didn't trust the lawyer for Dixon Holding, who promised that the Pile would be preserved. (It was leveled a few months later.) "What's all the land going to be used for anyway?" asked Roger. The lawyer said, "Recreational acreage." It had been a long meeting and everyone was exhausted and they adjourned.

But Roger googled the Dixon Trust and learned that the owner was a trucking tycoon named Dick Dixon who owned a fleet of 2,000 semis and a lot more. In 2018, Mr. Dixon had gotten a bee in his bonnet to run for Congress in Tennessee, challenging a right-wing Republican, C. J. Buzzhardt, in the primary. C. J. wanted to close the borders to immigration, require the wearing of flag insignia by every American over 18, institute the memorization of Bible verses in the public schools, forbid State Department employees to learn foreign languages, and require every federal employee to take a loyalty oath while hooked up to a polygraph. It didn't leave a lot of room for an opponent to run to the right of him, but Mr. Dixon did some intelligence work and got a video of Congressman Buzzhardt in a Starbucks, saying, "I'd like a latte light with soy milk and a sesame croissant, please, Stephanie," and he spent a million bucks to run that video on cable and Facebook along with a country band singing, "We don't need a latte light to fight for what we know is right, let's send a man from Tennessee to Washington, D.C." The way the congressman said "soy milk" and "sesame croissant" sounded definitely effeminate.

Congressman Buzzhardt was a fighter. He did some scouting around and found a video of Mr. Dixon at a charity ball, singing "I Feel Pretty" while wearing a blond wig and a summery dress and pearls. It was a fundraising stunt in exchange for someone donating $40,000 to a fund for muscular dystrophy, but he sang the song in a lovely falsetto with real feeling, and Buzzhardt ran the video with a deep voice saying, "Do you want a patriot or a patty-cake representing you in Congress?"

It was a tight race that went to a recount, and Mr. Dixon won by 160 votes out of 180,000 cast, so Buzzhardt entered the general election as an independent and he hit hard on the flag, the Bible, and true-blue Americanism, and secretly distributed pictures of Mr. Dixon wearing a blue surgical mask and head covering and gown. It went viral in the district, with the caption "Why does Nurse Nancy want your vote?" Dixon put out press releases pointing out that he was visiting his old aunt in the hospital and didn't want her to catch his cold, but explanations carried no water compared to the visual: he looked unmanly—he wore the gown with shorts underneath so it did look like he was wearing a dress—and to drive the point home, the video played "The Dance of the Sugar Plum Fairy," and he was whipped soundly and that was the end of it.

For a Bible-toting pro-life fiscal conservative, Mr. Dixon

had an interesting personal life. Three marriages and a couple of romances with bosomy singers with big hair working his Eldorado casino in Florida and a half-ownership of the cable channel NSFW and a personal friendship with the outlaw country artist Johnny Rogers. Quite a portfolio. Plus trips to Morocco for purposes unknown and 87 e-mails recently deleted to a woman named Hot Pants.

Dixon and Johnny had met by pure chance years before in the private-jet terminal at Nashville International airport, Dixon waiting for his Gulfstream, Rogers for his Bombardier, both headed for LA, and Dixon mistook him for Kenny Rogers, which Johnny didn't mind at all, and when Dixon found out he was the guy who wrote "Born to Raise Hell," he was thrilled. "My favorite song," he said, and he sang a couple verses.

I got sick of this old town,
No excitement to be found
Now everybody's telling stories
How I trashed the lavatories
When I walked by the fire barn
I saw the box with the steel arm
I broke the glass, I rang the bell
I raised hell.

You can see my writing on the wall
In every lavatory stall.
Set off sirens during Mass,
Threw a rock through the stained glass.

25

I done my job very well
I was born to raise hell.

Nobody in Nashville had done a song in praise of vandalism until then, and it was an odd song for a conservative Republican to love, but he really did, and they sang the last verse together:

One last time I saw your face
I had to rip up the place
Shot the lights on every pole,
Emptied every garbage can
You took up my time but not my soul,
I am a hell-raising man

Dixon's plane was delayed and Rogers said, "Hell, fly with me," so he climbed into the Bombardier with Rogers's road manager, Sam, and the band, the Trashmen, and they sat knee to knee all the way to LA and drank whiskey and talked politics, and Rogers wrote a song.

I used to be a Democrat
But I grew up and got over that.
No longer to the left I bow,
I'm a Republican now.
We'll fight Iran and the Muslim axis,
Lower confiscatory taxes,
We're all Republicans now.
Nuts to Europe and the rest of the world.

Got a hold of the trigger and our finger's curled.
Give us steak, I'm done with kung pao,
I'm a Republican now.

Dixon came along on Rogers's Hell-Raising Tour in 2008 after his No. 1 hit, "Driving Truck," with the famous refrain: *"Only thing I'd rather do than driving truck, And that's walk up to you and say, Let's—."* It was banned by every radio station in America, and that drove it to No. 1 and it stayed there. It inspired thoughtful opinion pieces in the *Times* about cultural decline, and when Johnny Rogers did his tour and played every racetrack in America, that was the song the crowd was waiting to hear, and every time he sang the refrain, 10,000 people shouted the rhyme and every woman raised her shirt. Tanker trucks of beer were sold, and the air was thick with illicit smoke. Every concert got in the news for the sheer number of public indecency arrests, complete strangers having sexual intercourse in the parking lots. When Dixon was asked about the song during his congressional campaign, he said, "If you don't like liberty, then you're living in the wrong country."

Liberty was the bond between the staunch Republican and the man who sang about vandalism, and when Roger Hedlund read about the Keep America Truckin' park on Dixon's Facebook page, he guessed it wouldn't be a wildlife refuge. The figure of 2.2 million visitors came from an architectural firm Dixon had hired and also the fact that the two high-rise hotels would be sited just behind Our Lady of Perpetual Responsibility church and next to Bunsen Motors. ("There's our buyer," Clint told Clarence. "We'll become a parking lot. It could be worse.") Roger talked to some of the neighbors of the Tingvold, Halvorson, Kreuger, Pfleiderscheidt, and Schroeder farms that Dixon had bought, and they admitted they'd been offered awfully good money for their property and they were weighing the offers.

"It occurs to me," Roger told Clint, "that if we don't move quickly, this town may become suddenly extinct."

Clint said that if Mr. Dixon offered good money to buy Bunsen Motors, he, Clint, would not have to think too hard or long before accepting it.

"What about Lake Wobegon? What about the rest of us?"

"Most Americans think Lake Wobegon is fiction," said Clint. "What's the harm in selling a piece of fiction?"

Clearly, the Dixon project was on the move. While the town had an epidemic of bad behavior to deal with.

3

GOD'S MISTAKE

A theistic pronouncements are a rare phenomenon in Lake Wobegon, rare as earthquakes or waterspouts, though of course the Norwegian bachelor farmers maintain their unbelief and everyone else has had their doubts, especially in the month of March, but Clint's outburst following Darlene's unbosoming followed by Liz's toilet seat story were talked about left and right, and when Lenny Olsson called up from Dallas, her mother, Ingrid, bent her ear with the news of strange events, and Lenny never got to talk about what she had called to say, which was that she'd decided to divorce Greg and quit her job in public health and drive north. She got her SUV lubed and the oil changed. She needed time to think things through.

Lenny's birth name was Elaine, and she graduated from LWHS in 1992 and decided she wasn't an Elaine but an Elena. She became a SPASM child (Simply Pray And Send Money) and enrolled in drama school in New York, but nobody from Minnesota ever did well in theater, theatricality goes against our nature, so she woke up, smelled the coffee, got into Athena College, tried philosophy, then took a biology course, which started her down the road to epidemiology, and, instead of sensational, she settled for smart. She was so smart and capable, you'd never imagine her life falling apart like it did, but Greg had gotten into the clutches of a folksinger whom Lenny hired to sing at his 50th birthday party, and she sang "Will the Circle Be Unbroken?" and suddenly he wanted to be in her circle and went on the road with her and Lenny had the locks changed and called a lawyer. When Ingrid regaled her with the news of town, Lenny said, "This sounds to me like a virus, a food-borne infection, like Mad Cow disease. People ate beef containing brain tissue infected with bovine spongiform encephalopathy, and they suffered personality changes as a result. Is there something going on with unpasteurized dairy products?"

And half an hour later she called back and said, "I googled 'inappropriate' and 'epidemic' and got a magazine story about Icelandic folk dancers who dropped their pants during bandstand dances, and the answer was a rancid cheese called Landsman cheese. Unpasteurized. Ring a bell?"

It rang a big bell. Hilmar Bakken. No need for Google. You say the word "cheese" in Lake Wobegon and people say, "Hilmar." He's made a religion of it. Cheese made the way it used to be made when Pasteur was but a child at his mother's unpasteurized breast.

Lenny is an epidemiologist, she knows her onions, and when Ingrid spread the word and said, "Lenny says it's probably a food epidemic, maybe cheese," it became authoritative. And people started to use the word "epidemic" rather than "This thing going on."

There was no mention of the epidemic in the *Herald Star*

that week nor news of large-scale farm sales to a billionaire in Nashville, though people were talking about it. The front-page story was GROWING SEASON WELL AHEAD OF LAST YEAR, SAYS COUNTY AG AGENT along with the school lunch menu and the town council minutes with several requests for zoning variances, and how to liven up your dinner table with colorful centerpieces made from egg cartons, and UNBEATEN WHIPPETS TROUNCE BARDS, 6-ZIP, about Ernie the old knuckleballer who had developed a screwball that bewildered everybody. He went into a corkscrew windup, ducked his head, turning slowly as if he forgot something and then lunged off-balance, and sidearm came the pitch and it rose and dropped and batters waved the wood helplessly, and the Whippets' catcher, Dutch Pfleiderscheidt, used a catcher's mitt the size of a fruit basket. Ernie was old and had back pain, and somehow his pain put extra backspin on the ball and made him invincible. He didn't tell anyone, but a pregame cheese sandwich gave him feelings of invincibility and when you feel it, you're halfway there.

Barbara Ann Bunsen heard about the epidemic and came home to check on her elderly parents, Clarence and Arlene. Her husband, Bill, didn't come; he gets exhausted from dinner table conversation about people he doesn't know, like coming into a class without having read the text. Clarence and Arlene pooh-poohed the epidemic idea, said, "It's a whole lot of hoo-hah about nothing. Darlene worked herself into a state of collapse, and Pastor Liz had a glass of wine before church that morning and she gets high on a tablespoon, and your uncle Clint is impressed by books he doesn't understand, so it's all smoke and no fire." Barbara Ann felt reassured and went jogging around the block, and the neighbor Florence who had never said more than "Hello" to her before stopped her and said, "I see you out here running and I understand that longevity is your goal and good for you, but what is the point of longevity if not to become a better person, and let me tell you, I look at your kids and I think you could spend less time in personal exercise and more time teaching them some basic principles such as respect for other people. You may be hot stuff in the city, but we have other standards here. I guess you look on your kids as God's gift to creation, but other people see two little snots who are cruising for a bruising. A word to the wise. Have a nice day." Barbara Ann was stunned. Arlene called her neighbor on the phone and said, "You can't talk to my daughter that way," and Florence had no idea what she was talking about. No idea.

One day, Cliff, the former owner of The Mercantile, came back from Minneapolis where he'd relocated after The Mercantile had been forced out of business by Amazon, and he sold the building to the county, which rehabbed it as senior citizen housing, 12 units, very nice if you like small rooms with very high ceilings. He told Irene, "I have to talk to you about something personal." They'd been friends since grade school. She invited him over for lunch. He looked good. His hair, which he'd been shaping for years with hair spray, now looked fairly natural. He was using the same facial bronzer but not as heavily, and his moisturizer made him look years younger, maybe three or four.

"I have to confide in you," he said. "You know I was very close to my mother." Irene nodded. "She was my best buddy, I knew I could always count on her. After she died, I wore some of her clothes sometimes to make myself feel better. Not her girly clothes but her bathrobe and her pajamas. I suppose some might think it strange, but it's nobody's beeswax, is it. But I'm 78 years old, and I have a secret and I'd like someone in Lake Wobegon to know it. I want to tell it to you."

"Of course," she said.

He said, "I think I'm gay."

"That's wonderful," she said. "Congratulations."

He said, "I've wondered about it for a long time, and I think I am. I like nice things. I like to dress up and go to shows. I love Barbra Streisand. I don't have a boyfriend and don't know if I want one, but anyway, I feel good about myself. Finally. And in Minneapolis, nobody calls me Goldilocks."

She said, "Well, I've always loved you and I always will and you know that." He said, "Yes, I know." She asked him if he'd been eating cheese from Bakken's farm, and he said no, he'd given up cheese years ago. "Good," she said. "It carries a dangerous virus."

Clint was reading up on atheism and appreciating the liberty that comes with dissent as compared to the burden of upholding orthodoxy. Nietzsche said, "Is man merely a mistake of God's? Or God merely a mistake of man?" Brilliant. Delicious. *I'm tired of being good*, he thought. *I've been lying on my back all my life looking up at Ford transmissions and coaching middle school basketball and grocery shopping for shut-ins. Let someone else do it, I did my share.* Napoleon said, "The main use of religion is to keep the common people from murdering the rich." So there was more to Napoleon than the hand stuck in the jacket. Deism offered people the luxury of self-righteousness while denying them the necessity of self-reliance. Look at the Women's Circle, which enjoyed lectures on the plight of immigrant workers, African-American artists, Haitian children, Iraqi Christian women, endangered species, the lack of capable violin teachers on Indian reservations, but when it came to concrete action, never did the rubber hit the road. Look at Donnie Tollerud, who suffers from Winter Attitude Disorder and belongs to a Christian WAD group, and even so he finds it hard to get out of bed and then when spring comes, he finds social interaction difficult. He needs certain nutrients that are found in beer, and he wears a button that says, PLEASE UNDERSTAND I AM DOING MY BEST. People with his illness need to live in Florida, but there would not be a support system for him there to respect him and not judge or ridicule, so he limps along, and the Women's Circle prays for him weekly, and what the young man needs is less sympathy and a good kick in the ass.

Back in early March, soon after the Men's Fellowship incident, Clint had a near-death experience when he was out for a walk by the lake with his dog, Fred, and saw a money clip on the ice about 50 feet from shore, and he tiptoed out and picked it up—there were five one-dollar bills in it—and Fred whined and tried to turn back and now Clint could feel the ice was rather spongy here, he took two steps toward shore, and his feet sank into the ice, and the dog looked up at him and Clint could see he was envisioning Clint's death, the loss of his meal ticket. Clint tried to stand lightly on the ice. His own death, happening before his eyes. He thought, *What a nitwit. Your dog is a genius compared to you.* He was wearing a heavy down jacket and if he went into the water it'd gain about a hundred pounds and he'd drown. He thought of crying for help, but in his state of levitation, the air he'd inhale might be enough to break the ice. It was Irene's fault. He'd had an argument with her when he left the house. She said, "What's with the jacket? It's 42 degrees out." But her contemptuous tone of voice obligated him to wear the damn jacket, which made her in a way responsible for his death, but of course after he died, she'd tell everybody, *I told him, I tried to tell him.* She'd be sad, but she was no martyr, she'd get over it. She'd sell his collection of Dan Brown first editions, his collection of every LP James Burton plays guitar on, sell the house, move to the high-rise in Fort Lauderdale where her sister Marlene lives, take up golf, find a guy who is happy to teach her to putt, stand behind her, arms around her, hands on her hands, and she'd tell him about the late Clint who died when he went through the ice and this Florida guy would laugh his big plaid ass off. Her infidelity pissed Clint off, and he strode across the ice and on his next-to-last stride he went through the ice, but the water was only two feet deep and he splashed to shore and walked home in a cold fury, but it was far enough to home that he got calmed down. He strode into the house and plopped down in the kitchen and said, "So? You miss me?" She said, "How come your pants are wet?" He said, "That dumb-ass dog ran out on the ice and I had to go out and get him. Thought I was going to go through the ice and drown, but I was lucky. What do you say we go upstairs and take a nap?" And he winked. "Oh, for mercy sake," she said, "I just took a shower and got dressed, you mean I have to get undressed?" But she followed him upstairs, complaining softly, and he kissed her neck about 20 times and

35

her bare shoulders and then descended slowly from there and they got into bed and then she didn't complain any more. They were in bed for an hour or so of sweet adolescence, and then he went downstairs naked and poured two glasses of Pinot Noir and took them back up to bed, and they lay together and talked. She said, "I'll never understand you." "Good," he said. She said, "Now that you're an atheist, we're having sex and drinking wine, and it's not even 11 a.m. What comes next?"

"Let's sell the house and move to Fort Lauderdale," he said.

She smiled. "You mean it?" she said.

"I want to take up golf." Actually, he wanted to find the guy who'd likely have married her and take him out fishing and throw him overboard in shark-infested waters with concrete blocks chained to his ankles.

He was pretty sure he'd met the guy. A yik-yakker in Marlene's building who had a great deal to say about power boats, the Second Amendment, barbecue, politicians he hated, why he'd never been sick a day in his life, the hoax that is veganism, the tragic decline of rock 'n' roll since the Kinks and the Who, and Irene and Marlene hung on his every word. Meanwhile the jerk's wife lit into him as they walked to the elevator. Clint heard her say, "Why is it you have to be the biggest asshole every time we go visit people?" and the man cursed her. Later, Irene told Clint that the Fenwicks had invited them to their church Sunday morning. "You mean, Mr. Fenwick invited you," he said. It was a relief now to think back to that night and realize the man was a churchgoer. Atheists have manners. They don't imagine they have the Supreme Being in their back pocket.

That afternoon Roger Hedlund found Clint in the Chatterbox, eating cream of celery soup and a Jell-O salad, red and green and blue and orange and gold cubes piled together—it was like a stained-glass window—and reading a book called *The Portable Nietzsche*."

"Neetchy," Roger said. "That was Hitler's favorite writer, wasn't he?"

"Hitler's favorite writer was Hitler," said Clint. "What can I do for you?"

Roger had uncovered a big fact about Dick Dixon, the trucking tycoon, why he bought up all that farmland. It was because Johnny Rogers came from here.

"From here? You're kidding. I never heard of him."

"He's from here. He was born Roger Johnson and the family lived in a little shotgun house on Taft, and the parents were at each other's throats and the dad was a drunk and the boy grew up puny and timid. When he was 11, his parents sent the boy off to live with relatives, and didn't get around to collecting him until he was 14. He had a stutter and was sent to a special school for the dim-witted, and one day he picked up a guitar and he got to where he could play in C or D or G, and suddenly he had friends and got invited to parties and girls looked at him with interest, and that was it. A cheap Sears Silvertone guitar. Dick Dixon owns it, and it's going to go into a Johnny Rogers museum. Along with his boyhood bedroom."

"Where'd that come from?" said Clint.

"The Rogelstad house. Formerly the Johnsons'. Dixon bought it and ripped out the upstairs bedroom. Johnson lived there until he enlisted in the Army and got stationed in Georgia and heard country music and, being as he was in the

Quartermaster Corps and his job was to count sheets and towels, he had plenty of time on his hands to play guitar and write songs. So that's his story."

Clint said he had no recollection of Johnson whatsoever.

"That's because you played sports and he sat in his room studying the Mel Bay Chord Book."

"But what's Dick Dixon's interest in making a big monument to him?"

"Simple. He has way too much money. And it's a tax dodge. And he wishes he could play guitar and sing and travel around in a bus. And Johnson's dead."

"What happened to him?"

"That's a long story," said Roger, and then Jack Bakkes, a man who goes for days without saying "Boo," walked up and put a hand on Roger's shoulder and said, "We're onto public employees like you. You've been at the public feed trough for years and nobody cared, but people are wising up to you and your golden-parachute retirement plans and the under-the-table stuff and the disability gold mine. Story in the paper the other day about a cop in St. Paul, twisted his back reaching for a jelly doughnut and strained a ligament, and he found a friendly M.D. and now he's pulling down 50 grand per year tax-free in disability, plus he got him a job as a security guard for 75 grand a year to sit at a desk and eyeball visitors, and on weekends he plays 18 holes of golf. But the free lunch is coming to an end, boyo, the people are going to rise up and take the sugar tit out of your mouth, not that I hold it against you personally, I don't, we've been friends since we were kids, but we just plain can't afford to put out the taxes the way we're doing in order to support country-club pensions for people who spent years putting in a 20-hour week."

Roger grabbed his elbow. "Get off the cheese, Jack, and come and talk to me a year from now and I'll explain it to you."

4

LENNY

Lenny arrived the next Monday in her red SUV with Texas plates and pulled up in front of the post office, and Mr. Bauser at the mail counter looked out through the bars and saw the tall woman in khaki shorts and red T-shirt and nothing clicked, no name, no address, though he'd coached her 4-H softball team 30 years before, so he resumed eating his chili and chips. Since his heart attack in December, he's been eating light and staying calm. The Benadryl helps. He got it for his German shepherd, Chief Bender, but Chief died of a hemorrhage last fall and now the postmaster is dosing himself, and it keeps him on an even keel. He used to get incensed at people who ask him what day it is, ignoring the calendar on the wall. Now he just tells them it's Monday.

Lenny was about to cross the street and then saw the ancient man pushing his walker past the Chatterbox. He stopped and glanced her way. She remembered Senator K. Thorvaldson, of course, the oldest man in town, now 99 and often unaware of who is who, but he has five very clear memories, each of which

41

he is delighted to talk about at length—the annual ice-cutting on the lake when blocks of ice were stored on beds of sawdust in limestone caves and used for refrigeration over the summer, the appearance of Charles A. Lindbergh in January 1936, forced to land his plane on a day so cold that when you spit on the ground, it sounded like you dropped a handful of dimes, and Babe Ruth's barnstorming tour with the Sorbitol All-Stars in 1938 and Babe driving his Cadillac town car that when he revved the engine and revved it again a flame six feet long blasted out the tailpipe, and the tornado of 1942 that blew a barn a quarter-mile with two small children inside who walked away unscratched, and the correct way to cure concrete, which they used to do and don't anymore. Lenny remembered that each of these reminiscences could take up to 15 minutes and sometimes lead to another and a third. The full set of five could go for three hours. She turned away to hide her face and looked at the front window of Bob's Barbershop and watched Mr. Thorvaldson's reflection as he waited for her to show interest and finally he continued on his way. Bob was not the barber anymore, Bill was. She remembered that Bob left town in 2009 after the infestation of ferocious black flies that ate holes in window screens. People dozed off in their porches and woke up to find their hair had been chewed down to the roots. Bill arrived in 2011 and kept Bob's sign because it was beautiful gold lettering and why pay money to be Bill, "Bob" was good enough.

Lenny crossed the street quickly and walked into the Chatterbox, which was empty at 2 p.m. on a Monday, and looked at the jukebox and saw songs she remembered from back when she waitressed there, "Third-Rate Romance (Low-Rent

Rendezvous)" and "Long Gone Lonesome Blues" by Hank Williams and John Prine's "Paradise." She sat down at the counter, where Cathy didn't recognize her. Cathy is the daughter of Darlene, the old waitress who quit her job after she threw the food at Daryl Tollerud.

"Hi," said Cathy.

"I'd love a coffee," Lenny said. "I've been on the road since yesterday morning. Left Dallas and wasn't tired, so I drove all night. Let me tell you, there are some weird people on the radio at two and three in the morning talking about left-wing conspiracies, but they do keep a person awake. I heard a healing prayer service coming through Missouri, and you could phone in your prayer request and your credit card number and he promised to heal you. I never heard prayer like that before. I grew up Lutheran, when we prayed it was pretty dry." "Okay," said Cathy. She didn't pick up on the invitation to converse. Lenny said, "Does Dorothy still own this place? I remember she used to serve the best waffles in the morning. And steak and eggs with hash browns. I never could make hash browns up to my husband's standards. So I guess I should blame her for the divorce." No answer from Cathy. But when Dorothy came out of the kitchen and looked around, she trotted right over, and Lenny stood up and they hugged. "Lenny, Lenny, Lenny, bright as a penny," said Dorothy. "I was afraid I'd never lay eyes on you again. How's everything in Dallas?"

"Horrible," she said. "A nightmare. That's why I'm here."

She'd come north while her lawyer started the divorce wheels in motion. She'd married Greg thinking he was someone he wasn't, and he tried to be who she thought he was and it

43

fell apart, as deceptions tend to do, and he took up with Sandy the folksinger, so Lenny came home to start planning her next chapter. Her cousin Debbie Detmer wanted her to come out to California, where she had a lucrative practice in veterinary aromatherapy and was active in a movement called Radiantism, which holds that *You find God by not looking for Her and letting Her find you.* Lenny was tempted to go. She was 45, her son was an actor working as a waiter and her daughter was trying to find herself as a Texas progressive, and meanwhile Lenny was curious about the outbreaks of nuttiness in town among people who'd been bottled up tight for years and now their corks were popping.

"We've been needing someone like you to figure it out," Dorothy said. "Clint turned atheist, Darlene tried to be a stripper, and the Lutheran pastor had an adventure with a toilet seat. We need a detective to get on the case."

That afternoon Lenny spoke to Mr. Sjostrom, the old geography teacher, who had buttonholed Clint Bunsen and told him that liberals in state government, financed by the Chinese, were sending death panels into rural areas, looking for people carrying Bibles and marking them for future harvest when they will be tranquilized and fitted with brain drives wired to follow commands from Beijing. He said that whole counties of North Dakota have been repopulated by humanoids who walk and talk like Americans but who are prepared, when the directive comes down, to seize the oil wells and the cattle ranches and turn the churches into union halls. He leaned in close: "Look around and see who uses soy sauce," he said. "That's the giveaway. Mind-altering chemicals. It's so obvious that nobody notices."

When Lenny spoke with him, he said his diet was whatever Dorothy served at the Chatterbox. Except for a bucket of home-made cheese he bought from Hilmar Bakken that reminded him of the cheese his grandma made. Lenny made note of it.

She spoke to Dorothy, who'd had her own incident while waiting on Clarence and Arlene at Sunday brunch and throwing a couple napkins down on the table and yelling, "I get so friggin' sick of working my fingers to the bone to keep this dump open. One of these days, I'm going to burn the place down for the insurance and let people drive 15 miles to a Burger King and live on their greaseburgers and frozen fries and watery shakes and you won't have me to kick around any longer. I'm history. Going to find me a little motor home and get lost in America." She didn't remember it, but when asked about cheese, she reached into the cooler and pulled out pounds of it, she called it Portuguese cheese, her cousin Hilmar made it, and she sold it as a favor to him. "He's been making it since Jesus was in the second grade, and yes, I have eaten some myself, when I've felt depressed."

"What sort of cheese?"

"Portuguese cheese. It's got reindeer milk in it. He keeps two of them and they have babies in the spring and he milks them through the summer and fall. It reminds a lot of people of the cheese their grandmothers made. It has a real zip to it."

So Lenny decided to go see Hilmar. "His farm is three miles south of town. You can't miss it," said Dorothy. "Big sign, 'You Are Not Welcome.' He means it so drive slow and be ready to hit reverse. He's taken a shot at me a couple times after I'd bought a new car, but his eyes are so bad that his aim is poor."

Lenny was, of course, aware of Hilmar, having grown up here. He was spooky, with his rampant white hair and rancid smell and raggedy clothes. A living example of why men need women: for basic maintenance. Like most Norwegian bachelor farmers, he was a contrarian. If you said the sky was blue, he'd look for a cloud. She knew all about the tribe. The NBFs are descended from Norwegian villagers who came to America to escape from respectability and maintain the tradition of public drunkenness, dirty songs, and blowing their noses by hand onto the ground, one nostril at a time. They use handkerchiefs to mop the brow, not to blow the nose. (Why would you rub snot on your forehead?) You plug a nostril with a finger and with one mighty snort empty the other nostril onto the ground, which makes city slickers feel faint. Thus you clear nasal passages and achieve exclusivity at the same time. The bachelors sit on the bench by the Sidetrack Tap like old snapping turtles in the sun, foreigners in our midst, who've never been parents, never been required to set a good example, so they don't bother. They are pessimistic anarchists, so nothing dismays them. They come to church twice a year to satisfy their deceased mothers, sit in back and don't recite the Creed or the prayers and doze through the sermon. And sometimes they go outdoors and blow their noses. Moral disapproval is not a factor in their lives, so people don't bother.

Hilmar was the youngest of seven, lived at home with his mother, Irmgaard, was a decent left fielder, sang in a barbershop quartet called The Hay Makers, bathed in the stock tank, and then in 1985 when his mother died, it tipped him over the edge. He stayed home for two years, half his teeth fell out, he put up KEEP OUT signs. The Bakken farm is 60 acres, a dozen Holsteins, a flock of chickens, two reindeer, plus a pack of wild mutts. He preserved the farmhouse exactly as his mother had left it, and he moved a mobile home onto the property for himself. He kept to himself, became cranky and ill-mannered, put up the angry signs along his driveway, but Wobegonians feel a proprietary affection for the NBFs: they are malcontents but they are ours, our crazy uncles, and who will take their place when they are gone? Nobody. They'll be gone, like the buffalo.

The next day, Lenny drove out to visit Hilmar, bringing a quart of Everclear 190-proof grain alcohol as a gift. She'd heard the gossip about the Nashville man buying land for a trucker park and she drove into the Tingvold farm next to Mr. Bakken's and it was abandoned, the back door open and the kitchen bare. And then she heard the blast of a shotgun. She drove next door to Hilmar's with the big sign, YOU ARE NOT WELCOME. And another sign by the mailbox: YOU HAVE NO AUTHORITY OVER ME. Fifty feet farther, NO KIDDING. Along the driveway, a series of signs:

DOWN WITH BUREAUCRATS! FREE THE PEOPLE!

FOR GUN CONTROL, I USE BOTH HANDS

EVERY MAN HAS THE RIGHT TO BE WRONG

YOUR LIFE IS NOT MY FAULT

Beyond the windbreak, a little white farmhouse, a few wrecked cars in the yard and an old green mobile home with Brother-hood of Liberty painted on the side. As she pulled in, barking dogs came dashing from all directions and jumped up on the car, two on the hood, fangs bared, snarling deep in their throats, and then a man shouted, "Haul up!" and they slunk back into the bushes from whence they'd come. The man approached, shotgun cradled in arm, an old gaunt man with ball-bearing eyes, black coveralls. She rolled down her window.

"You're not from here," he said.

"I used to be. Lenny Olsson. Married a Huston but I'm back to Olsson now."

"Ollie and Ingrid's girl."

"Right."

"What brings you out here?"

"I heard about your cheese, and I'd like to buy a box."

"Who told you I sell cheese?"

"Dorothy at the Chatterbox."

"Fifteen bucks. I only take cash."

"You got change for a twenty?"

"I might."

He walked toward the farmhouse, and she followed him. She noticed the two reindeer in a corral adjoining the chicken coop, shedding clumps of winter fur. He opened the farmhouse door, and she followed him in. She expected it to be junky, but it was orderly and neat, a sofa with antimacassars on the arms, a rocker, an old radio, a crank telephone on the wall. The cheese was in the kitchen. The counters were clean. The refrigerator appeared to be from the early '50s, a Frigidaire. He smelled okay to Lenny. Dorothy said he only bathed for Midsummer's Day and Christmas Eve, but she was wrong.

"I was sorry to hear about your mother's passing," she said.

THE LAKE WOBEGON VIRUS

"She died upstairs. Thirty-five years ago. I took care of her to the end. People in town thought I should've put her in a nursing home. I would've shot her before I did that and then shot myself. You want to see the upstairs? It's just like it was."

She said, "Oh, that's okay." She was afraid she might go upstairs and find a corpse on the bed. "Some other time," she said.

The cheese was in a wooden box the size of a child's shoebox. It was grayish, under a transparent film.

"Why do they call it Portuguese cheese?"

"A misunderstanding," he said. "It's Norwegian cheese but it's called that from French portagers. They loved it because it keeps the mosquitoes off you. They had mosquitoes the size of hummingbirds. You could die from the bites."

"Oh really—?"

"Really," he said. "You eat a spoonful every day, and you'll never need mosquito spray. The portagers were scared of mosquitoes, that they might carry disease, so to them the cheese was worth more than money. It was the portager cheese that enabled the French to come inland. Otherwise they would've kept to the coast, and the Vikings would've taken over. The English were no match on the open seas. They were a nation of shopkeepers. The Vikings were the warriors. But the French had the cheese."

"That isn't the history they taught us in school," she said.

"Exactly my point. Schools are run by the government, and they teach you what they want you to know. Goddamn government is a gang of collectivists who send the USDA and the milk inspectors in to regulate every tiny detail of life along with the liquor laws and zoning regulations and the weed control people and drug laws, to where it gets so that a man can't breathe, can't turn around without there's somebody there saying which foot to put in front of the other. Young kids grow up nowadays with no idea of freedom. None. They're like cattle in the chute. People who stand up for their rights, we're a dying breed. Big corporations, big government, it's all the same psychology, and it's meant for poultry, it isn't meant for me or you. Anyway, that's how I see it, and when you're on my land, then you can see it that way too."

He smiled slightly. She handed him a twenty. He opened up a tackle box and rummaged around in it for dollar bills. "I sold milk for years to the Avon Creamery and thought nothing of it, and then I heard on the Liberty Network news that pasteurization is a European rule meant to soften the soft palate for the pronunciation of French vowels and there is evidence that pasteurized milk is connected to a lower sperm count and the physical timidity of young men, and I asked about it and right away they got suspicious and sent out inspectors and found that I was milking the reindeer too, and they read me the riot act and threatened to take me to court, so I switched to making cheese, which my mother had done, and I still had her recipes and her wooden cheese forms. And it sells darned well. Gammelost. Old Cheese. Pasteurized cheese has no flavor, like everything else these days."

"What's in the cheese?" she said, and the moment the words were out of her mouth, she knew it was the wrong thing to say. He smiled. He looked at the door. The visit was over. "Give my best to your folks," he said.

Lenny took the cheese back to her parents' house, and her mom took one sniff and said, "You've been out to Hilmar's."

She said, "I don't get what people see in that cheese. They say it reminds them of their grandmother's. An outhouse reminds me of my grandmother, but you don't see us build a two-seater out back, do you? No." Lenny wrapped a slab of cheese in plastic and sent it to a laboratory in St. Paul, and Mr. Bauser took the package and said, "Technically you're not supposed to ship cheese by U.S. mail, but I'll make an exception this one time."

Meanwhile, the outbreaks continued. Bill the barber went on a tirade against the U.S. Senate, and why should states like North and South Dakota, Montana, Kansas, Nebraska, and Wyoming have as many senators as New York or California, they ought to be run by the Bureau of Land Management, all while he was cutting gashes in Ernie's hair for emphasis. It wasn't the conversation you want from a barber but Ernie was brought up not to interrupt so he didn't.

Clarence saw Tom Hanks on a TV in the Bunsen showroom and had a fit about celebrities and their big social causes like global warming or endangered species or pollution by plastics, and he yelled at Hanks on the screen: "You're an actor. So be an actor. Who cares what you think about saving the rainforest? Go live in the rainforest if you think it's so great. Grow your own food. Build a tree house. Make friends with the crocodiles and learn their language. I don't give a rip. So you feel guilty about owning three houses and having a gazillion dollars. Give it away if you feel bad, but spare me the righteousness." Clint didn't say a word, but he noticed the cheese dip on the hospitality table and sent it over to the Sidetrack Tap, and Clarence calmed down. Clint stopped at the Sidetrack on his way home, and Wally was talking about his grandpa who as a young man had bred a three-legged chicken that appeared in *Look* magazine, which impressed his girlfriend, Valerie, though the chicken was unable to walk and had to live suspended in a sling. His grandpa then designed artificial wings to attach to the chicken to enable it to enjoy independence, and he was close to success, having experimented with a man-sized pair of wings made from turkey feathers and attached to a harness. He had flown from a barn roof and the wings worked pretty well, and meanwhile he was struggling with the ethical question—Did the chicken truly wish to fly or was it happier in its sling, and what right did he have to decide this for the bird?—but he put on his wings and climbed to the top of the windmill, which was turning slowly in the wind, and he was drumming up his courage to jump when he heard a motor and looked up, and a biplane with cloth wings piloted by a man in a brown leather helmet and a long white scarf was landing in his pasture. Valerie, who was waiting to see grandpa fly, ran out to meet the man with the white scarf, and he offered to take her up for a ride and she said yes. Grandpa did not jump. He threw the wings off, and he climbed down and walked to town and went into the tavern and broke his promise to his mother and had a glass of whiskey and it was the cure for everything. He was surrounded by friends who got friendlier and friendlier and some women too, and there was music and cribbage and a buffet of snacks, and he was completely happy and that's how Wally's family got into the bar business. "What we learned from that is that you can go ahead and dream, but if your dream doesn't come true, consider yourself lucky, something better is on the way. Flying is okay, but friendship is what it's all about." Wally had finished all the cheese and was licking his fingers.

That evening, big black thunderheads moved in from the west, sheets of rain swept across town, the sky exploded into light, bolts of electricity ripped into the earth, thunder slapped against the houses, six inches of rain fell in two hours, rain poured down the gutters and out the spouts. For the storm lovers in town, it was blissful. Maybe they secretly wished they could bust loose themselves and a big storm was theater for them, an imitation of life as it could be. Storms can be dangerous and most people seek cover, but if you stick your head out the door, you'll see spectators here and there who are enjoying the storm and cheering it on. A sign blew loose from the old Mercantile building and went clattering down Main Street, a 4-by-6 sheet metal sign that said, QUALITY TAILORING ON-SITE, INQUIRE WITHIN, which hadn't been true since 1948, but the sign was saved for the hand-lettering and as history. The wind said *To hell with history* and sent it flying, and it bounced off the Sidetrack Tap and what if a patron had wandered out the door and been decapitated by QUALITY TAILORING? It didn't happen, but it was worth consideration. Barbara Ann Bunsen sat in her BMW with her three teenagers who moments before were engaging in heavy eye-rolling sarcasm about fat people in dumpy clothes walking by, but now they were terrified and they whimpered, "Let's go inside, please. Please let's go inside." And she got to be the tower of strength and say, "Don't worry. It's only a storm." Dispensing false reassurance to your terrified children who will soon go back to mocking Myrtle's horrible black wig and purple blouse.

But this town looks good in a bad storm, it's when you see why the town was formed in the first place. Shelter in the storm. The prairie was prime for cultivation but there are no hills to hide behind. People gathered together in towns to feel less vulnerable and they were determined to stay put and get along with their neighbors, no matter what. Strange to see a cheese product eat away at the foundation of civilization, but that is exactly what was happening. Cheese caused a social ferment that drove people apart.

5

THE AUTHOR ARRIVES

I came back to town in late March, parked on Main Street, and walked around. I hadn't been back since the funeral of Aunt Dot, where I commingled with my cousins, avoiding talk about politics or things I'd written about them in the past or my third marriage, then in its 20th year. Divorce is uncommon in my family, same as going over Niagara in a barrel. It is considered unseemly and is to be avoided by the simple means of selective inattention. Aunt Dot stayed married to Uncle Bud even though he had a horse laugh that ended in a hearty snort, a laugh that startled strangers and small children, but she found a way to overlook it and focus on his good points, his tenderness and generosity, his good workmanship. And she carefully avoided saying anything funny. He was a good man—so what if he whinnied? Aunt Sal stuck with Uncle Eldon though she taught English and Eldon commonly began a sentence, "Her and me brought you a present"—"Her and me are going to Florida this year"—and rather than spend her life correcting him, rather than shooting him, her ear learned to block it out.

My beloved cousins had stayed true to the Sanctified Brethren tradition that they and I were raised in, and they faithfully attended the Gospel Hall north of town for the Breaking of Bread on Sunday morning and the Wednesday Bible reading, whereas I had fallen by the wayside into a deep ditch, seduced by the lures of the Episcopal Church, Catholicism with a small C, a pageant of costumery and smoke and candles and ancient liturgy, whereas the Brethren relied on truth and truth alone. They spoke directly to God and He spoke to them, whereas I was a spectator at a play where a man in a golden robe and a tall hat sprinkled some water on me and made me feel good. In Minneapolis I was a respectable citizen, but when I come to Lake Wobegon, I am a pagan and a writer who told stories that people here would prefer were kept quiet, and I have done it for money. This is treason and thievery. The first memoirist was Judas Iscariot: he wanted the Book of Judas to come out in Latin; 30 pieces of silver was his advance. An old friend of mine, a distinguished old man, a leading citizen of town, when he and I were young, sent away for a pair of binoculars that could see through girls' clothing. The binoculars were a gyp, but along with them came a packet of French postcards of nude women, rather shadowy and blurry but nonetheless interesting to him and his friends. I was a nice boy and did not wish to bring shame upon my family, so I had never seen pictures of naked women, only some half-naked African women in *National Geographic*, but I only glanced at them, did not stare. They carried jars of water on their heads, bundles of straw, kindling wood. I didn't study them closely. Some of them had wooden discs in their lower lips and some wore rings in their noses, or sticks inserted through the middle cartilage. There were many interesting things about them other than breasts. But I looked at his French postcards when he offered them, and it was thrilling. The female form is a fundamental aspect of the natural world, and why should it be kept secret so that a young man, on his wedding night at the hotel, seeing his bride step out of the shower naked, might be alarmed by her splendor and panic and go home to his mother? I stared at his pictures, and he and I planned a swimming party. We were 14. We stole vodka from his house, and we invited six girls and four other boys. We met at the lake and had some vodka, and he suggested we all swim naked. We boys stripped, all except Chuckie, and we dove in the lake, but the girls stayed on shore and swiped our clothes and sat on them, and we were pleading with them: *You promised. Hey. You promised. A promise is a promise.* The girls laughed and laughed. And he and I slipped away in the dark and we locked the outhouse, as a way of evening the score, and Donna Bunsen, who had urgent needs, came out, banged on the door, then ran into the woods, about 10 feet from us, and squatted and hoisted up her swimsuit and a river came out of her, and when she was almost done, I said, innocently, "I never saw a girl pee before." Which was the truth. She screamed and let out a huge fart, and I said, "I never heard a girl fart before either," and she ran back to her friends, sobbing, and from then on, I was a criminal, a Peeping Tom. We hadn't locked the door with voyeurism in mind, but it was interesting to see what we saw, and I said so and he kept quiet. He was there in the bushes with me, and I know it and he knows it. But he was popular and I was an odd duck, and so I was considered a voyeur with an obsession about girls peeing. A little incident

57

like that sends two people down different paths in life, him into real estate and law, me into writing fiction. After that I exercised great discretion. I went away to college and enjoyed the company of educated women and never heard any of them expel bodily gases—nor did I wish to, I had already been there and heard that—nor did I take an interest in their urination procedures. Eventually, I found a girlfriend who was just as eager to lose her virginity as I was to lose mine. It was our third date. She asked, "When are you going to make love with me?" I didn't make her ask twice. But back in Lake Wobegon, I was considered a possible pervert.

I walked down Main Street, braced myself for hostile looks, but instead was shocked by how the town had changed. I had tried to preserve it in my stories and now I saw the reality. It was like going to Pompeii and finding a Walmart. The Alhambra Theater is a seniors center now—old men look up at the gilded ceiling and remember where they sat when they took liberties with their girlfriend and then glance across the table and there she is, 78 years old and glaring at you as if you were thinking dirty thoughts, which you haven't for years. There is an ATM now at the State Bank; Old Man Ingqvist despised the idea of doling out money, no questions asked, but he died, and a month later, in it went, over his fierce posthumous objections. The Sons of Knute Lodge was sold to Dittman Fitness, and now people ride stationary bikes where once the Grand Oya presided over the Earls of Trondhjem in their robes and polar bear pelts. The Knutes came to an abrupt end with the Depression generation; nobody born after 1940 wanted anything to do with fraternalism, the gilded throne, the old Norwegian songs, the elaborate rituals, and the bowing and turning, the oaths and swords and scepters. Art's Baits & Night O' Rest Motel became Allied Self-Storage for people to keep their junk in, a morgue for useless stuff you can't bear to part with. The statue of the Unknown Norwegian was moved from Main Street because people were sick of explaining to visitors that it's not a war memorial, it's that nobody knows who the guy is, a tall dignified man with glasses and mustache who was well-known once and then wasn't anymore—and then a dirty word was painted on the Unknown's chest that Bud worked two days to clean off and did clean it off but it was still there in people's memory. *Dumbass.* It was permanently blighted. So now he stands in front of Bunsen Motors with "Our Founder" painted on his chest; he was made family and that took care of the problem.

Jack's Auto Repair is gone. Jack didn't approve of automatic transmission and refused to work on automatics, and he eased into retirement that way. You'd walk by and see him under a car up on a hoist and listening to "It Don't Mean a Thing If It Ain't Got That Swing." He was a good mechanic and specialized in hopeless cases and he loved jazz, everything up to and including Ellington. The place was sold to Krebsbach Chev for storage. I walked by the joint and the silence was mournful, the music was missing.

The fire barn is the same, except the warning notice is gone from the front door. Art had his office there. He lived for snow-plowing, and in the warm months he took out his frustrations by leaving warning signs in the park: "DON'T DRIVE ON THE GRASS. HOW MANY TIMES DO I HAVE TO TELL YOU?" "NO CLEANING OF FISH ON PICNIC TABLES. IT ATTRACTS BEES. NO EXCEPTIONS, WHERE WERE

You Brought Up? A Barn?" And an enormous hand-lettered sign on the door of the fire barn:

> Doorbell Is Broken. I will fix when I get around to it. So if you push the button and I don't come to door, that is why. don't get your undies in a bunch. If there is an emergency such as a fire (Duh!) pull the alarm, don't ring bell. As I said before, it is broken. When will it be fixed? I don't know. I'm waiting for parts. It's complicated. Rome wasn't built in a day. And don't offer to fix it yourself, I have been down that dead end before. P.S. If you have read this notice all the way to here, you maybe need to find something better to occupy your time. P.P.S. Do not remove this notice, it is here for a purpose. Thank you.

Bob's Barbershop is next door where Bud liked to hang out when he wasn't putting up notices, or he'd go to the Feed & Seed and talk to Ernie's wife, Ella, about vacation disasters that justify staying home. Detwiler's Drugs is still open with the bins of jelly beans and licorice and caramels, the Lake Wobegon *Herald Star* with the display of engraved wedding invitations in the front window, the sort that were popular 50 years ago, and Ralph's Grocery with the sign in the window, If You Don't Find It Here, You Can Probably Get Along Without It, and Lundberg's Mortuary in the big white mansion with the pillars out front. (Cremation services are available on request but not advertised, cremation being regarded as atheistic.)

The mansion used to be the Thanatopsis Society, whose members are long departed to their reward. I am old enough to remember hearing those ladies' voices reciting the last lines of William Cullen Bryant's poem "Thanatopsis":

So live, that when thy summons comes to join
The innumerable caravan, which moves
To the silent halls of death, thou go not, like a slave to his
dungeon, but, sustained and soothed by an unfaltering trust,
approach thy grave, like one who wraps the blankets about
him, and lies down to pleasant dreams.

They ended every meeting with that group affirmation of mortality. On paper, they were Lutherans or Catholics, but by joining the Society, they became secret humanists who believed in human goodness, contrary to the teaching of their parents. The Society sprang up in Victorian times among strong-minded women who kept their opinions to themselves. Men were not admitted to the Society. They were not wanted. The Society did not seek equality for women, it assumed women's superiority.

Mrs. Hoglund was in the Society, she of the silk blouse and hair coiled on her head, her glasses on a chain hanging across the great promontory of her bosom as she taught her pupils from the bright red John Thompson piano books. She played piano at Society meetings, a Chopin étude to start, and then she accompanied the crowd in "All Things Bright and Beautiful" or "Whispering Hope." But Chopin was the dividing line. Women could feel Chopin, men could not. On a May afternoon, you could walk around town and hear her pupils practicing for the recital, playing Chopin, and the girls felt it and the boys made it sound like a fight song. Chopin is not about fighting, he's about losing. I never had piano lessons. We Sanctified Brethren believed in discouraging the talented lest they acquire a superior attitude and encouraging the modest so they'd be able to accompany hymns but no more than that. I can whistle a little bit of Chopin but not much. I lost my chance to play Chopin, it's gone forever, and that's why I love his piano music so much.

My grandma, Dora Powell, was a Thanatopsian. She said, "No woman should ever have to depend on a man. For sustenance or inspiration or anything else. Let the man go his own way. The woman has power over the children and that gives her influence over the future. Things are inevitably heading in the direction of justice and mercy and the love of beauty." What broke up the Society was higher education. Young women went to college, which prepared them for careers in one narrow bureaucracy or another, whereas the Thanatopsians considered themselves Philosopher Queens, not technicians, not managers. When my wife, Jenny, says, "The arts is what separates human beings from the beasts of the forest. If you do not respond to beauty, you are lacking a soul," she reveals herself as a Thanatopsian.

It was a shock to see my grandma's temple of the arts turned into a mortuary. Where Orrell Holman lectured on Newton's Laws and Catherine Jacobson paid homage to the transcendentalists and Lavona Person read Louisa May Alcott and women pledged themselves to lifelong learning and the advancement of the arts, now Mr. Lundberg pumps formaldehyde into dead bodies and turns them into mannikins. This is a shock to memory. Imagine if you went to Washington to see the sights and there's what you remember as the Supreme Court building, and the banner, MUSEUM OF FREAKS & ODDITIES, 500 MUMMIES ON FULL VIEW.

I walked around the Prairie Home Cemetery, looked at my family's plot, the empty space next to my parents. Did they want to be that close to me? Uncle Jack, who was on the other side of the empty space, could recite whole passages of scripture by memory backwards, verse after verse, every word in reverse order. It was quite astonishing. I don't believe he was a believer, but he knew his Bible, some of it anyway. Father Emil's grave is there under a modest stone, Emil Dworschak, 1924–2020. He asked to be laid to rest among Lutherans where he might do some good. Bud Mueller, the old snowplow man, is next to him. Bud drove a 1957 Dodge dump truck with an Allis-Chalmers plow on front and he made himself irreplaceable by virtue of refusing to allow anyone else to look under the hood. It snowed eight inches the day before Bud died, and he got out of bed and raced around town throwing a wave of snow onto the driveways and sidewalks, burying cars, practically immobilizing the town, and drove home and gave up the ghost. His coffin lies under the old snowplow blade: Mrs. Mueller felt that, in a heavy snowfall, Bud might try to rise from the dead, and the blade is meant to keep him in place. The old town clerk, Viola Tors, is there, a serious mistake on her tombstone—she died in 2016, not 2006, and the stone company says it'll cost $750 to replace the 0 with a 1 and it won't look right anyway, and the church runs the cemetery and takes a "Who cares?" approach to the problem, but it is a serious offense, to erase 10 years of a person's life. Viola was a stickler for accuracy. Her daughter, Eleva, and her daughter, Deb, are in anguish over it. "Grandma would roll over in her grave if she saw it," said Deb. "Well, tell us if she does, and we'll go calm her down," said Irene, who is on the church council. "The stone company says if we fill in the zero and write in a one, it'll look trashy, like a typo correction. Look at it this way. Viola gets to be 10 years younger."

I ran into Lenny as I left the cemetery and said hello. Her older sister was a friend of my younger sister. She asked if I'd been eating cheese, which I hadn't. "We're having some food poisoning here, so be careful," she said. I asked how things were in Dallas, and she said, "Greg's in love with a little tiny folksinger named Sandy. Jeans with holes in the knees, blouse with pearl buttons, hair down to her thighs, sandals, the whole deal. He met her when I hired her to sing at his birthday party, and now she's got her hooks in him. He went into our IRA to pay off her credit card debt. He quit his job at Apple and became her road manager, driving the motor home and selling CDs at the coffeehouses she plays. So I called a lawyer, and between me and the kids' college fund, Greg is about to be skinned alive. Sandy sings about poverty, and now Greg will get to experience it firsthand. So everything's great. How about you? What brings you to town?"

I told her I came because my classmate Marlon asked me to write a brief for my friend Sister Arvonne of the Sisters of Benevolent Persuasion, who died in 2016, for her to be beatified and achieve sainthood. Marlon needed to prove miracles accomplished by her since her death. He and I were two uncool kids and we had been provisional friends in school so he asked for my help with beatifying Arvonne. But that wasn't the real reason I came. I came to escape humiliation

I moved to Minneapolis right out of high school and strove to be cool—strove, struggled, studied coolness, imitated assiduously, learned the language, adopted a look and kept updating it, wrote satire, became a monologuist, and in 1985 was one of *Playgirl's* 10 Sexiest Men in America, while Marlon combed his ducktail, worked on the old cars in his yard, yelled at his wife and kids, ran the Municipal Power Plant. He was in charge of repainting the water tower, and he spelled the name *Woebegone* on the paper he gave the painters, instead of *Wobegon,* a mistake that got on the 6 p.m. news in the Cities, a big joke, a town that can't spell its own name, and he made the mistake of giving an interview in which he said, "There's more than one way to spell a name"—in other words, his uncoolness had grown with time. And he'd run the Arvonne sainthood proposal through spellcheck but there were many mistakes left, *bad* instead of *bade, flour/flower, heel/heal, angle/angel, lie/lay, its/it's,* and dangling modifiers, subject-verb disagreements, and so forth.

I ran into him a few years ago at a class reunion, me the distinguished author and sexy American, him the town misspeller, and we exchanged hellos, then two years later, someone shot a video of me sneakily trying to clear my left nostril while trying to look like I was scratching my nose, latching on to a dry clot of mucus that was attached to a long gob of mucus and I happened to be wearing a scholarly robe and sitting on a platform at the Harvard Phi Beta Kappa program, about to be introduced as their keynote speaker. The gob was enormous and I had to yank my decorative hanky from my breast pocket and grab the gob with it, but it was awkward and indelicate and unmistakable. This video was stitched to one of me cleaning wax out of my ear with a pencil and one of me reaching up under my suit jacket to pull my underwear out of my crack—1 minute, 45 seconds, of public humiliation, which went up on Facebook, then other platforms, got two million hits, then three, then four, and I became an instant meme, Mister Pickett, and all my coolness was gone forever in one big whoosh, like flushing while seated, and a vast aggregate of people were given the chance to feel superior to me. I wanted to go hide out someplace where people aren't so tied in to social media, and I thought, *Lake Wobegon.* Not much Twittering up there except in the trees in the spring, la la. I needed a month or so to accommodate myself to the fact that I've lost whatever cool I worked half my life to acquire. In my hometown, I can sit in the cafe and have coffee and someone might ask about my grandpa and when did he arrive in town (1880) and is it true that my grandma was a railroad telegrapher (yes) and how many children were in my mother's family (13, including her), but nobody is going to say, "Was that you I saw online at the Harvard Phi Beta Kappa?" My people have a long memory for hometown events, but the Internet is a river at flood tide and it flows over the rapids and nobody remembers what it looked like yesterday.

I remember a man my age named Ivar Ingqvist, who was Hjalmar's brother and might've taken over the Ingqvists' bank but he got in an argument with a man from Millet over tomatoes that Ivar was entering in the county fair tomato contest. The Millet man said they were store-bought, imported from Mexico.

Ivar said he was crazy. They yelled at each other and the man challenged Ivar to an arm-wrestling match, and Ivar rolled up his sleeve and put his elbow on the table and the Millet man put his down and word got around town—people came running from all over. The table was in the tavern, but it got too crowded so they moved it out in the middle of Main Street and there were hundreds of people crowded around, and more arriving by the minute. Two big fellows in red flannel shirts, elbow to elbow, wiping their hands, applying talcum powder, and Mr. Thorvaldson was the referee. Some boys arrived from band practice with their instruments. Mayor Pete Peterson was there and led the crowd in the Pledge of Allegiance. And finally, Ivar and the man from Millet locked hands and the referee slapped the table and the men strained, their shoulders swelled up, their backs bent, their faces turned red as tomatoes, sweat poured off them, the crowd was watching, breathless, minute after minute passed, the combatants were forehead to forehead, panting, first Ivar had the advantage, then the Millet man, and suddenly a young woman laughed and that's when Ivar let a fart. It lifted him up out of his chair. It sounded like a powder keg blew up. People hit the ground. It smelled something fierce. Women fainted and a couple of men. And it took the starch right out of Ivar and the man from Millet pinned his arm and threw his head back and laughed, and the crowd applauded, and Ivar slunk away in humiliation.

He joined a traveling carnival as a champion pie-eater, and after the man who juggled cats and a woman who could belch nursery rhymes like "Jack and Jill went up the hill to fetch a pail of water" and a balancing act using milk bottles and bowling balls, Ivar came out and ate three blueberry pies in one minute without spilling on his clean white shirt. The carnival went from town to town, and Ivar took college courses by mail and got his B.A. in history, graduated with a 4.0 average, did a master's at Yale, started an investment fund, earned a fortune, lived in a penthouse on Fifth Avenue in New York, married a Columbia professor, they had four kids, spent a good deal of his fortune helping aboriginal tribes in Kenya develop their lands, he wrote a book about it, and years later he came back to Lake Wobegon, which was pretty much as it had been but nobody recognized him when he walked into the Chatterbox in his Brooks Brothers suit and wingtips. He ordered the Hot Beef Sandwich, and it came and nobody walked up and said, "Hey, Ivar, long time no see," and then he heard two men arguing about the Lake Wobegon Whippets and one of them said, "I haven't been to a game in years, they haven't had a winning season since I was a kid," and the other man said, "No, they had a winning season the year Ivar Ingqvist let that fart." He came home to find that he was a historical marker in town, like a famous battle or a flu epidemic. He paid for the sandwich and got in his car and drove away and never returned. In New York, he was a great and good man. In Minnesota, he was an expulsion of gas.

I walked around town, and some people nodded and said hello and others didn't seem happy to see me. They give me credit for having married well, but that does not erase their misgivings. Alice walked straight up to me and jabbed her finger at me and said, "You're going to write a book about this, aren't you, and make us look like a bunch of nincompoops."

"Write a book about what?" I said. "I'm here to work for Sister Arvonne's sainthood."

"Sainthood, my aunt Sally. You know damn well what I'm talking about, don't pretend you don't."

"I don't," I said but now I was getting interested. I figured it was the bad cheese epidemic that Lenny had mentioned and the incidents of free speech.

"You go around giving talks in New York or wherever and making fun of your hometown, and when you need more material, you come tiptoeing back and take notes about flamingo lawn ornaments or meatloaf or Bingo Night or whatever and go write a book about us hicks, and don't think we don't know it. All your sophisticated readers get to feel superior at our expense and you collect the dough and what's in it for us? Tell me that."

I told her that I am only a working journalist and I report what I see and hear to the best of my ability.

"Best of your ability—well, there's the catch right there. How about if I call you a backstabbing scuzzbag and sleazeball? You want to put that in your book?"

"If you'd like. If that's how you want to be quoted. But don't say it unless you mean it."

"Do I need to spell it for you? S-c-u-z-z-b-a-g." And she turned on her heel and stalked away.

So I started taking notes for this book. A man has to have something to occupy himself and the Sister Arvonne project was hopeless. She was a saint in my opinion, but the Catholic Church has its own requirements, such as miracles. Google is a miracle, so is FaceTime, and they're accomplished by armies of diligent grasshoppers, not by saints. Saints love their neigh-bors, abstain from cruelty, serve the poor, and do it cheerfully. The miracles Marlon had assembled, such as the boy who was drowning and had a vision of Arvonne telling him to relax and take a deep breath and put his head back, were unremarkable: the kid had simply remembered her teaching him to float. No miracle there, just attentiveness. Most of the evidence of saint-hood was along the lines of *She was a woman whose great exam-ple made me the good person I am today.* Her sister nuns testi-fied to her sense of humor; her sister Lois said Arvonne had a delight for children but that's not about sainthood, it's about goodness. Arvonne was a Hoerschgen and grew up on the fam-ily hog farm near town, the rebellious daughter—her parents were Lutheran and she read Thomas à Kempis's *The Imitation of Christ* in high school and at 17 entered the nunnery of the Sisters of Benevolent Persuasion, known as the Purses because they carried large handbags full of good books. They believed that faith is simple common sense. "Videtur ad finem," was their motto (*Think it through*). The best argument for her saint-hood was the miracle of the wildflowers. She had planted them in her parents' pasture and after her death they bloomed in early February, rising up through the snow in full color, long before anything else. The Hoerschgens built a stone wall around the flowers, and it had become a prayer station where women, even unbelieving women, came to kneel and pray for their men to behave decently, but there was no evidence of miracles, unless you count softening of heart and apologizing and other small reformations.

Marlon said they asked for my help because I know important people who could get the word out. "My important people are all Jews," I said.

"How about journalists?"

"The reporters I know are the ones who write obits."

"Well, do your best," he said.

That was what brought me to town last March. It wasn't to write this book. Writing a book was the last thing on my mind. I wanted to get off-line, off Facebook, stop getting messages from people saying, "I think you're in this video." I wanted to be who I am for a change, not who four million people think I am. But as long as I was here, with time on my hands, I started writing about the virus.

6

STICKING AROUND

Several times I almost got in my car to drive back to Minneapolis and didn't because I dreaded being alone. The Mister Pickett video from Harvard had cut deeply into my self-esteem. Especially the scene of me trying to get my underwear out of my crack—it looked like I was scratching my ass, not what you'd expect of a Phi Beta Kappa speaker, and the viewer comments were deadly: *This is why we have bidets.* And: *It's not there, sir, it's on your shoulders, right in the middle.*

My self-esteem had shrunk to a wisp of a shred. I needed love. My wife was on an opera tour in Japan and Indonesia, doing *Der Rosenkavalier,* playing viola in the orchestra, gone for a month. Our daughter was in school in New York, leading her own life. I had been looking forward to staying in Lake Wobegon with my cousin Betty, who was a psychology major and knows us relatives better than we know ourselves. She told me once, "Your problem is that you're trying to live four lives at once and a person can only live two." Another time, she said, "You're a difficult man in a happy life and I am a happy woman in a difficult life." I love these crisp analyses of hers and I needed her help in my current state of despond, but now she had flown off to Montana to see to a friend who'd stuck her head in the oven because her neck was wrinkly and ropy, and Betty had left me a key to her house under the doormat. So maybe there was no reason to stick around. And it hurt that Alice had given me the hairy eyeball and was in the Chatterbox warning Clarence and Wally and Dorothy not to talk to me unless they wanted to be made fools of. I saw her in there, gesturing, glaring at me through the window.

So I walked into the cafe. It was a brave move. I am not a brave man, but I decided not to accept being slandered in my hometown. I know about slander and there's not a lot you can do about it. When you've written a best-selling book, people are overjoyed to find a video of you picking your nose. So let them enjoy it. A man doesn't need to have thousands of admirers, a dozen true friends is enough. I walked into the Chatterbox, past the table where Alice stood, saying, "The chickens shouldn't go to the fox's church and sensible people do not make friends with a cruel satirist." I walked past her, she watched me pass, and I headed for the end of the lunch counter and who should I see there but Julie Lyngdal, now Julie Christensen, who smiled at me and I smiled back and sat down next to her. It was just as simple as that. I reached for a menu and she said, "The meatloaf is good today." So I ordered that. She was eating a piece of apple pie. "How are you?" she said. "Never better," I said, and I meant it.

This is why I go back to Lake Wobegon. For all that's changed, you can turn a corner and suddenly it's 1957 again. We talked about mutual friends, our kids, the news, whatever whatsoever, and then she said, "I always meant to write and ask you for that poem you wrote for me."

So she remembers. Good. A man would want the first girl he ever kissed and meant it to remember, and she does. It was in October. Our lockers were near each other. She told me after school one day that she liked the poem I'd written, that Miss Fleischman had me recite in English class, a poem that begins,

The leaves of wonder are falling
Under the old oak tree
And I wait for someone to come
and watch them fall with me
and I wonder who she shall be.

She asked if I made it up or if there was a real oak tree. I said, It's in a little ravine out by Moonlight Bay, so we walked over that way after school, she was carrying her books and I wished I were *American Government*, which was the book pressed to her left breast, and indeed there was an oak and a pile of leaves under it and she said, "I love leaves," and she sat in the pile and I sat next to her, and then we were lying in the leaves and the books were set aside and then we had our arms around each other. She asked what I would do when I grew up, and I said I would become a writer. She said, "Then I should give you something to write about," and she kissed me. Lightly but with feeling. I kissed her back. We lay back, contemplating the gravity of the moment. We talked about other things and then we went home.

We went back to the oak tree every afternoon, three in a row, and we lay in the leaves, arms around each other, and kissed, and

I put my hand over her breast. And the third day she said, "Why are you so sad?" And I didn't have an answer for that. I didn't know I was sad, or "so sad," but if Julie Lyngdal said I was, then I must be. And the next day she couldn't come to the oak tree because she had cheerleading practice. I felt rejected, but I wrote her a poem. *I just kissed a lady named Julie in a pile of leaves fallen newly and that kiss shall remain through sun, snow, and rain, a treasure clearly and truly.* She read the poem and thanked me and kissed me. I don't recall what happened later. But she is still a beautiful thought in my mind. I didn't need to talk about it and we didn't. She said, "It's nice of you to come help with the Sister Arvonne campaign. A couple of old nuns are excited about it and it gives them something to do. And if you find that poem you wrote, send me a copy."

So I stuck around. I went to Betty's, slept on her couch, hung around town, and after a couple days, people accepted that I was there, no comment necessary. I became part of the landscape, a piece of furniture.

I was sitting quietly in the Sidetrack when Mr. Berge told a tale, obviously untrue, about trying to catch a giant walleye he calls Gloria with his new Amazon rod and reel and he cast the line and she took the hook and yanked the rod out of his hand and she dove and he yelled, "Alexa! Where's she hidin', Gloria" and Alexa played a Haydn Mass, the Gloria. It was Berge's usual fish fable, but it inspired Barb Diener to tell about the time she left her husband, Leroy the town constable, and upped and drove off to Minot, North Dakota, and registered at the Minotaur Spa on the banks of the Souris River, and Leroy found the letter she'd left for him saying she would file for divorce on

grounds of emotional desertion because he was so uncommuni-
cative—he'd spoken 14 sentences in two and one-half months,
she had counted—and he'd gone fishing on their 25th anniversary and gotten drunk and slept in his car and come home at
6 a.m.—no apology—and asked her to make him waffles with
blueberries. Leroy drove to Minot and went to her room and
was about to knock when he heard a man cough and Barb say,
"Are you okay, honey?" and it broke Leroy's heart, cop though
he was, to think she'd already found someone else, so he went
back to his car to shoot himself. He put the .38 to his forehead,
then thought, "No, I want to do this in front of the two of them
so they'll remember it" and went to her room and she opened
the door and there was her dog Doug—it wasn't a man's cough,
it was a dog's—and he opened a beer and told her the entire
story of his life from the orphanage to his adoption by Adolf
and Trudie Diener and his service in the Navy and his season
with the Whippets, batting .340 until the night game in St. Rosa
where a whole bank of lights went dark in the top of the 7th and
the ump said, "Let's play ball," and a ground ball was hit sharply
to Leroy and took a bad hop and struck his forehead and ever
since he'd had a hard time forming predicates and he prayed for
the disability to go away and it did the moment he read her note
about the divorce. He talked all the way from Minot to Minnesota about his love for her. He redid their bathroom and put in
a steamroom. He took dozens of portraits of her nude and hung
them in the dining room which her family didn't know what to
say about and kept their eyes on the food, not glancing up. She
told the whole story as she ate her mac and cheese. Astonishing.

Clarence and Arlene sat and listened to her—what choice

did they have, sitting six feet away? He'd ordered a cheese-burger with raw onion, which brought tears to his eyes. They are a happy pair. They were high school classmates and acted the lead parts in the senior class play, "Romeo and Juliet," which she remembers and he doesn't. Their biggest argument is about leaves. He burns them, and she mulches. He prunes his lilacs in the fall, and she composts hers. Hers look better, but they don't talk about it. He loves chicken liver, she considers it loath-some: why not eat the pancreas and gall bladder too? He avoids yik-yakkers, she likes talkative people. She is very big on birth-days, he isn't. He turned 80 in January and sensed preparations being made, and he tried to leave town that morning but she'd taken the distributor out of the engine and put a potato in the tailpipe, and then the guests arrived and blocked the drive-way, all the jowly geezers he'd gone to high school with, and they sang "Happy Birthday" in their horrible ruined voices and Arlene served a beef roast with a fresh but experienced Cabernet and old-timers woofed about how busy they are in retirement and gave him dumb birthday cards ("Welcome to the Inconti-nence Hotline . . . Can you hold, please?") and a cake blazed up like the *Hindenburg* and people told him how youthful he looks, which they never said back when he was reasonably good-look-ing. Hours later, after the guests left, she asked if he'd enjoyed it, and he said, It was like being thrown in a swamp to be attacked by badgers. She cried and slept in the guest room that night, and in the morning he apologized sincerely and thanked her. She forgave him. She fixed him steak, medium rare, and fried eggs over easy for breakfast and she put her hands on his shoulders and kissed his bald head and said:

Give me my Romeo; and, when I shall die,
Take him and cut him out in little stars,
And he will make the face of heaven so fine
That all the world will be in love with night
And pay no worship to the garish sun.

And that was the end of it, no more was mentioned.

It was pleasant to be there, unnoticed, paying attention, a shadowy figure in the corner. I turned my hearing aids up so I could pick up distant conversations. Nobody bothered me except Alice, and she gradually came to accept my being there. I like not being fussed over. In Lake Wobegon, people know as much as they care to about me and don't necessarily care to know more. I'm sure that, in my obituary in the *Herald Star*, somewhere in the third or fourth paragraph, it'll mention something about my having written books, but there won't be reference to accusations of an indiscretion, meaning Donna Bunsen the urinator. And if there is, so be it. A life without indiscretions is hardly worth the trouble.

Lenny doesn't know about my bad reputation, she is 20 years younger than I, she never listened to my radio show, she's only read my limerick book and is lukewarm about it, and it felt good to talk with her and know I was in the clear, no expectations. She was worried about her mother, who is showing signs of losing it mentally, and Lenny feels she should sit down and make peace with Ingrid and apologize for old misunderstandings and bad feelings. "I don't want to be angry at a crazy person," she said.

I told her to talk to my cousin Betty. Betty has the answers.

"Do you have unfinished business like that?" she said.

79

"I know people who are angry at me, but now they're losing memory capacity and the anger is still there but rather amorphous since they can't remember my name."

"So you have no unfinished business to take care of up here?"

I don't know what made me tell her what I told her then—it had little relevance to anything, but it was on my mind, and she asked, otherwise I never would've volunteered it. It was about my trip back home in 1969 when I dropped out of grad school, a story I've never told before because I'm not clear on one crucial detail—whether the woman's hair was red or black—and I want to be definite about that. Let's say it was red.

It was September, 1969, I was enrolled in a Melville seminar and I started reading *Moby Dick* and hated it. Call me Ignorant but it was dull as dishwater, so I got a radio job at KSJR in Avon, east of Lake Wobegon, and headed up there. I was driving a red 1967 Mustang, and 10 miles south of Avon I saw a hitchhiker with a hand-painted sign that said, Lake Wobegon. I didn't recognize him, but I stopped and he got in. He wore a stocking cap and a heavy black coat and his face was turned away. He said he had come back after a long absence to find his family. He directed me toward the woods on the east side of the lake. "It was a happy home," he said, "with picnics and card games and the family singing around the piano, but something bad happened and my father left home and we were generally ostracized by others and so I ran away. It's a long story." He said, "You wouldn't happen to be a Keillor, would you?" I nodded yes. "The one who went away to be a writer?" "Yes," I said. He directed me down the road around the east side of the lake, to a narrow two-rut track into the woods, with bushes growing in it, and I drove along, slowly, feeling the underbrush scrape against the undercarriage. I'd never gone that way before. When I was a kid, riding my bike around the countryside, we avoided that road because there was a story about a man who'd come out of that house and gone downtown to the Chatterbox and asked for codfish and Dorothy said, "We haven't served codfish since I've been around, sorry," and he walked away and left a paper sack and in it was a pearl-handled double-barrel derringer and a copy of the St. Paul *Dispatch* with a front-page story about a suicide. The paper was from June 1928. The ink was fresh.

And now I saw the house, which we knew as the Spangler house, a brick manse with a copper roof and high pointed peaks, a wrought-iron fence around it, all rusted and falling apart, and the front door hung loose on the hinges. In the downstairs hall hung a half-rotted painting of a beautiful woman with dark eyes and long red hair. The hitchhiker said, "My aunt Martha. The man who painted it was her husband, a fine artist who supported himself by bootlegging in the '20s. He ran a fleet of fast cars carrying whiskey down from Winnipeg. He hired beautiful women to be his drivers, beautiful women who could play poker and shoot straight. His wife stayed in Chicago, but one day she came up here to surprise him on his birthday and found him in his birthday suit in bed with a beautiful girl and his wife shot the two of them and herself and the bodies were buried in the cellar and the sheriff never came out because nobody reported the crime." The hitchhiker said this in a whispery voice that gave me the creeps. The place was heaped with trash, covered with dust and leaves. He headed up the stairs and I followed. He stopped halfway up. He said, "Sorry the place is such a mess, but when she found out he lied to her, it destroyed her spirit. He was a painter and she supported him and stood by him in his time of need and it broke her heart that he took up with loose women." On the landing, the hitchhiker put his hand on a doorknob for a long moment and I desperately wanted to run and not follow him in but couldn't think of what to say by way of an excuse. (*"I'm sorry, I forgot I left my codfish on the stove."*) He opened the door to a bedroom full of heavy, dust-encrusted spiderwebs, where the carcasses of deceased bats hung who'd been partially devoured by spiders, and there were two black spiders the size of sparrows with bright green eyes sitting on a wreck of a bed, half-rotten and collapsed, a blanket with a map of Minnesota on it, "Lake Wobegon" marked in silver. I looked beyond the bed to a mirror on the wall, and there was my reflection and not the hitchhiker's. I turned to see him behind me as he reached up and took his stocking cap off, and long red hair fell out. He was a she. She said: "I'm sure you don't remember—why would you—but today is the day I died in this room. I shot her and then him and put the gun to my head and swore an oath that when I was dead, I would roam the world avenging myself on all who have been unfaithful. You can protest your innocence—I'm sure you have stories to justify your sins, but I can see through every single one of them, just as you can see through me. So don't waste time in explanation. You're guilty as hell, and hell is what you're about to see up close. Your privileged life is over. Prepare to meet your judgment! God have mercy on your soul." She reached behind the door and pulled out a long wooden scythe with a curved wooden handle, and I dashed toward the window, running through the forest of dusty webs and the bodies of bats, thrashing my way through the filth and decay, and dove through the window onto the porch roof and rolled off and onto the ground and hit the ground running, covered with dusty webs and bat bodies, and even though my ankle was broken, I ran all the way back to town in a crazed panic. I didn't stop to try to find the car keys. (I found them in my jacket pocket an hour later.) I walked into my parents' house. Nobody was home. I stripped off my clothes and threw them in a paper sack. I took a long hot bath. I burned the bag of clothes. I got a ride to Avon and went into radio. Now, 50 years later, I wonder if my car is still parked there, with my college textbooks in the front seat and my knapsack and my journal. I need to find the 1967 Mustang because after all these years, I've come to doubt the story myself, and there's only one way to prove it. So whenever I get up the courage, I've got to look for that car."

Lenny looked at me in silence for a long moment and said, "I want to come with you when you look for it."

"Thank you," I said.

She said, "I didn't believe you at first—the hitchhiker and all—but when you got up to the bedroom, I thought to myself, *This man is a professional writer and if he were lying, he would've invented a better story without so many clichés in it.* Yes, I want to come with you."

First, she said, she had to figure out about the cheese. She needed to straighten things out with her mom, but once she'd taken care of business, she said she'd come with me to the old Spangler house. I felt good about that. When you venture into the spirit world, it's good to have a scientist with you. I was also astonished that I'd told that whole story to Lenny. It made me wonder what kind of cheese I'd been eating.

7

THE CHEESE BAN

The next Sunday, Father Wilmer preached on the story from the Gospel of Mark in which Jesus heals the woman who touched the hem of his garment. Jesus says, "Daughter, your faith has made you well; go in peace and be healed of your disease." We are all broken, we are all unclean and unfit, said Father Wilmer. He said it with great conviction. He seemed to be referring to himself.

After Mass, standing in the doorway, shaking hands, Father saw Megan Schoendienst and he put a hand on her shoulder and apologized for spilling wine on her during Communion. He said, "I have to confess that I was looking down the front of your dress and my imagination got away from me. It reminded me of when I was a boy and a girl named Virginia Schafer and I used to dance in her living room. I am a priest but I am still a man with carnal desires, and I hope you can forgive me." Her mother overheard this and snatched Megan away and told Father Wilmer that she would report him to the bishop, and that afternoon, a black Chrysler parked in front of Our Lady and the bishop himself strode in without knocking and angry shouts were heard and Father was ordered to pack his bags in 15 minutes and come along and Father did not, he packed a bag and slipped out the back door and down the alley to the Krebsbachs and Carl gave him sanctuary in his woodworking shop and after half an hour the Chrysler drove away. Carl took supper out to the shop and Father Wilmer was sitting at the table, sipping a cup of tea. "What happened?" said Carl. Father said that he was plagued with carnal thoughts when the weather got warmer, and he was no longer able to hold them in. He heard the words coming out of his own mouth and was astonished. "Was cheese involved?" Carl asked. Father nodded. "Lutheran cheese," he said. "A gift from a neighbor."

Lenny reported to Mayor Alice about her encounter with Hilmar and showed her the cheese. It smelled like somebody's old underwear. Lenny said it was a long-standing Scandinavian tradition, to serve an appetizer so foul that you ate heartily the rest of the meal to get the taste of the first course out of your mouth. She had read in Norse mythology that Viking warriors were fed rotten cheese to prepare them for battle and some had ecstatic visions from eating it and danced their way to the battlefield, which terrified the Celts and Saxons—"In other words, loss of inhibition due to food-borne infection became a tactic in battle. The Vikings came to America, had no interest in real estate because they were sailors, but they ate cheese and were fearless and danced with the Iroquois and the Narragansett, and the French portagers got it and it protected them from diseased mosquitoes and the West was settled," said Lenny. "But why would anyone eat it today?"

"You're young," said Alice. "You're accustomed to frozen

pizza and microwave dinners. Old people have been complaining about processed food for years. It tastes flat and meaningless to them because it's produced for kids who are full of allergies. The average 20-year-old has no sense of smell or taste. This is what antihistamines have done. My kids don't get excited by smells. Fresh coffee, new-mown grass, a bouquet of flowers, they don't notice. Home cooking means nothing to them. The difference between real chicken and factory. They want McDonald's, which is food for inmates. But old people miss the pork from pigs slaughtered on farms, same as they miss homegrown tomatoes and wild berries. It's not going to be easy to shut down Bakken's cheese. He's got a widespread secret clientele who have a love affair with his cheese."

"Do you eat it, Alice?"

Alice stiffened. "Yes, but I've been off it for almost a month." She started to say something, stopped, and then said it. "I walked into the Bon Ton to get my hair recolored and something reminded me of a scene in a movie—an old Western—where Lucille Ball walks into a beauty parlor and gives a speech and I did the whole thing—I said: 'It's been two months since the men went away and already you can see the improvement. No more garbage in the streets. No loafers and drunks lounging around. And yet—I miss having men. Miss the helplessness of them.'" And Alice looked around and she sang:

I miss the way he talks
So sweet and low,
He says, "What'd I do with my socks?
I had 'em a minute ago."

He's going to take me to the dance
Or to the picture show.
He says, "Does this shirt go with these pants?"
I say, "No."
He says, "You're awesome. You're colossal.
Let me kiss you."
And I point to his left nostril
And hand him a tissue.
I get along alone as best I can.
But I miss my man.

Lenny said, "And that's from eating cheese?"

Alice nodded: "I walked in doing the scene and Charlotte looked at me and said I looked flushed and made me sit down. I felt a glimmering around my eyes and my lips felt numb. It hasn't happened again. Thank goodness. But it was an exciting moment. I liked what it did to me. So, yes, I've been there and know what it's like. I know what we're up against."

They agreed that the issue needed to be addressed by the town council, though two of the council seemed to be on cheese themselves, Louie and Judy. He had announced that the Postal Service was opening and reading his mail and he was getting strange phone calls late at night from people with distinct Asian accents wanting to know his Social Security number. Judy had quit the PTA in protest against its accommodation of Harry Potter books despite their clear satanic underpinnings. She had highlighted devil worship in several of the books and the school showed no interest.

Sometimes the town council met privately in executive session because if it were an open meeting, people couldn't say what they really think. So Alice and Margie and Senator K. met at Alice's house without telling Louie and Judy. Senator K. is the swing vote and has no idea what's going on half the time, and usually he takes his cue from Alice, though sometimes he confuses Judy for Alice, they have similar hairdos, so there's that to worry about.

The executive committee agreed that bad cheese needed to be banned in order to keep the peace, and to save time, they'd do it without Mr. Bakken present, so Margie arranged for her daughter Carla to take her fourth-graders out to the Bakken farm to look at the old farmhouse he kept in memory of his mother who had dearly loved children, and they arrived Wednesday at 4 p.m. as the full council was gathering. Mr. Bakken's feelings about children were similar to his feelings about the income tax, but to make Irmgaard happy he allowed the children to touch her antique appliances, the woodstove, the crank phone, the icebox, as, back in town, the council stripped him of his God-given right to sell or give away his Gammelost.

First on the agenda, before they came to cheese, was Clint's annual plea for the Fourth of July: "I'm just going to say this: the Fourth has slipped into a pitiful state, and it's a tragedy because this is a great country and an inspiration to the rest of the world and yet the great day has gone into decline, except for the fireworks, and why? Because in a free country you can't make people celebrate freedom. Half the time you can't even get them to exercise it. And that's why it's important for us to keep this celebration going. Put on a parade and the Living Flag and a corn roast at the very least." No reaction from the crowd. Alice moved for further study. All the members nodded.

Then, without naming names, she described the incidents of hostility in town, and Lenny spoke about viruses and the danger of eating unpasteurized dairy products. There was a vaccine that might be effective, but one of its side effects is sleepiness and that is something Lake Wobegon can do without. So the council voted to ban unpasteurized cheese pending a report from a laboratory. Louie and Judy voted no, and Alice and Margie Krebsbach voted yes. Senator K. looked at Alice in bewilderment and she nodded and he voted yes.

As a matter of public health, the Lake Wobegon Town Council has voted to institute a ban on the sale of unpasteurized dairy products, particularly cheese, until we receive a laboratory report on the safety of consumption and its detrimental effects on public behavior. Your cooperation is earnestly requested. It is in the public interest to maintain standards of civility in our social intercourse. We hope to have further information in a month or less.

The notice was printed in formidable black type with the town seal (*Sumus Quod Sumus*) and posted in the *Herald Star* and at Ralph's and the Chatterbox and copies were mailed to registered voters, and two days later, the protestors showed up at the town hall and the town clerk, Viola Tor's son Vic, heard a clamor outside and went to the door and saw a crowd of a dozen or so, shouting, *We stand up for liberties, the right to speak and eat our cheese.* They wore cheesehead caps and carried signs, "The mayor is not a king in a palace. Up with liberty, down with Alice." Louie was there and his wife, Doris, and some Schoendiensts and several of Lenny's cousins and Dorothy's son Kurt and his wife and Dutch Schultz and Ernie and some of the Sidetrack Tap crowd. Vic listened to their complaints and advised them that a recall election requires a petition signed by 400 registered voters. As to the legality of the council's ban, he had no authority to comment.

Kurt was the most reasonable spokesperson, arguing that freedom of diet is basic to adulthood. The state and federal governments have the power to outlaw dangerous foods; a municipality does not. People's fondness for raw cheese is a matter of taste, like a fondness for lutefisk or fried eel or steak tartare. As for the "aberrant behavior" cited by the council, these are incidents of speech protected by the First Amendment. Louie had more to say about the collectivist mentality behind the ban, but Kurt was quite level-headed. He himself did not eat raw cheese, he said, but he needed to defend others' right to do so. "First they come for the cheese, then they ban the burgers."

Vic was polite but he's lived here all his life so far, and when he looked at them, he remembered that Kurt was the worst third baseman in history, a sieve, and his wife and Judy had once dressed up as shepherdesses for a school talent show and sung *Mairzy doats and dozy doats and little lamzy divey, a kiddley divey too, wouldn't you* while tap-dancing. Not the sort of people you look to for advice on public health issues. As for Charlotte, when she was 14, she wanted to switch from piano to trombone so she could be in band. Her mother said, "Honey, I hate to say it, but girls don't play trombone." And that sealed the deal and Charlotte, disagreeable by nature, became a dreadful blatty trombonist, clueless, tone-deaf, but a proud marcher. This is the problem with not leaving home: people remember all the bad stuff about you and it undercuts your moral authority.

The cheeseheads headed for district court in St. Cloud and challenged the town council's ban on unpasteurized cheese. They persuaded Louie and Judy and other lunatics to stay home, and Kurt presented their case as a matter of civil liberties and Alice asked for a delay so that Lenny could be present to testify. She was home sick with the flu. "She been eating the cheese?" said Judge Larson. He thought it was hilarious and so did his clerk. He talked about his own fondness for Norwegian cheese, and he discovered that he and Kurt had something in common, grandfathers who brewed their own beer in big wooden buckets, so the hearing slipped into reminiscence and beer appreciation and beer-drinking contests, and then the judge approved Kurt's request for a 90-day restraining order against enforcement of the ban, and that was that. The case was continued to a date in July.

From St. Cloud, the protesters drove in a six-car caravan to Hilmar's farm, where he stood in his yard and welcomed them and they purchased 40 pounds of raw cheese in affirmation of their rights as American patriots, and they held an eat-in at the farm, with cheese on homemade bread, and they sang:

The cheese stands alone,
The cheese stands alone.
We're free to eat the cheese
Any cheese we please,
The cheese stands alone.

They threatened Margie with a boycott of Krebsbach Chev and threatened Alice with impeachment and confronted Clarence and Clint and said, "Whose side are you on?" Louie said, "If you don't think we have the intelligence to know what to put in our own mouths, then I don't need to shop here anymore." They distributed signs to shopkeepers: WE SUPPORT FREEDOM OF CHEESE, and some shops posted them in the window and others didn't. Dorothy did. Then she crossed out "We" and wrote in "I." The Chatterbox is the center of public life in town, and maybe someday there will be sectarian cafes for people of various persuasions, but meanwhile everyone needs to feel welcome. And after all, she is Hilmar's cousin.

The problem with protest movements in small towns is that people know each other much too well, and Louie was not the brightest bulb on the Christmas tree. He didn't have the brains that God gave geese. People remember his adventure with the weather balloon and the helium tank. His brother had bet him he couldn't get off the ground and he took the bet and attached the helium hose to the balloon and it got bigger and bigger and up he went. This happened on Midsummer's Day, which used to be a big thing in Lake Wobegon. People gathered to drink and celebrate and they used to say:

Midsummer's Day, Midsummer's Day,
Say whatever you want to say.
A day of dancing and drinking and laughter
And all forgotten the morning after.

Louie was hanging on to the balloon but he couldn't get the

helium hose off it, and he went up pretty fast and he pulled out a knife and tried to poke the balloon but couldn't quite reach high enough. He was about a hundred feet up in the air and was sailing in a westerly direction over the trees and still rising. Some people looked up and imagined what they'd say if asked to give the eulogy and not much came to mind. His pants started to slip off him and he reached down to pull them up and poked himself with the knife and dropped it, and he looked like a goner and then a gunshot rang out and he began a slow descent. It was his mother. She had never shot a rifle before but he was her son and she felt a duty and put a hole in the balloon at almost 300 feet. He landed on a barn roof and let go of the balloon and it, with helium tank attached, flew up into the air. They raised a ladder and he climbed down, and she walked over and said, "Louie, you are dumb enough to be twins." He was speechless, terrified. He'd gotten a fortune cookie the night before that said, "You are about to experience a major life change." And he thought the life change might be death. But no, the life change was his marriage to Doris six months later. She was a good cook, and two years later he weighed 300 pounds and helium balloons held no more fear for him.

He was a joker. He saw an ad for a talking toilet seat and installed it in his bathroom and when Doris went into the bathroom, Louie put his ear to the keyhole, and when she sat herself down on the toilet, a man's voice yelled, "Hey, get offa there, I'm working down here." And the next thing Louie knew, Doris came galloping through the door and rammed the doorknob into his ear and he had a headache and blurred vision for two weeks afterward. But he'd spent a hundred bucks on the toilet seat, so he installed it in the women's toilet in the town hall, and Alice changed the message to Louie saying, "Hi. How's it going up there?" which she got from a voice mail he left, it was her joke.

The council took up the cheese issue once more. Louie and Judy weren't speaking to Alice and Margie, and Senator K. Thorvaldson spoke to everyone but not always with relevance, and when Alice stood up and proposed hiring a municipal therapist to ease people over the ill feelings the epidemic had caused, the cheese caucus walked out in a huff, so the motion passed unanimously.

Clearly, there were hard feelings in town that needed to be dealt with. Daryl didn't go in the Chatterbox anymore after the run-in with Darlene; he'd been a regular. The Lutheran church lost several lifelong members after the Pastor Liz incident. And then the town was shocked to the core when Father Wilmer was defrocked. The bishop ordered him to contemplate his sins at an abbey in Iowa, but instead Father went civilian, rented a room over the drugstore, took a mail-order course in barbering, and was saving up to buy Bob's Barbershop and go into business. He was excommunicated by the Benedictine order, but he'd been a good priest and of course he still had many friends in town, Lutherans too. In fact, he went to Pastor Liz for counseling.

"You should go talk to a therapist—Alice is bringing one to town," she told him.

"Nonsense. What would she know about us?" He told Liz that he suffered from phobias, the fear of crowds, the fear of being alone. And theophobia, the fear of God. Scared in the pulpit, scared at night in the rectory, and afraid God is going to

punish him for being a lousy priest. He was torn by insecurities
and it was too late to quit, he'd been priestifying for years. "I
was rebelling against authority but now I was the authority. It
was a mistake that got out of hand. My mother wanted a priest
in the family and I did it for her, and now I'm glad she's dead
so she won't know what a disgrace I am." And he broke down
and wept, and Pastor Liz put her arms around him. And it
occurred to him, clinging to her, what the deal was. It was a simple physical reaction. Nobody had hugged him in years. *Years.*
He couldn't remember the last time. Something about the collar
and the black outfit says: *Please, No Hugging.* By God, he was
done with celibacy. It had worked for a while, but now he was
done. He was a 57-year-old virgin and he knew nothing about
dating or women or how to talk about these things, but this was
the next chapter for him, he knew that. Pastor Liz could sense
it too. She gently released him and said she could not help him
on the next part of his faith journey, but she knew of a website,
Padres Seeking Partners.

He said, "Do you think that by any chance Lenny—or is that
crazy?"

She said it was crazy.

He had been replaced at Our Lady by Father Powers who'd
been attached to the Cathedral in St. Paul, an excellent golfer
whose mission was to play golf with Catholic tycoons who were
thought to be considering large-scale beneficence. Father Powers's unique gift was his ability to match his partner's game
stroke for stroke, to shoot 71 or 134 as needed so that he could
walk alongside Mr. Moneypants and chat about churchy matters
but in a chummy way, no preachiness. He admired businessmen

for their directness (*How much did you pay for this?*), and many a rectory roof had been repaired or retirement home added onto with dough he had finessed between the 10th and the 14th holes at St. Anthony's, the archdiocese course where the sand traps had thorns and some water hazards gave off steam. Father Powers was a faithful opponent of the reforms of Vatican II, which had cheapened the Church, protestantized it. He loved Latin and often slipped into it while saying Mass, turning his back to the congregation, as in the old days. He could be very frank about the failings of the hierarchy: the archbishop couldn't preach his way out of a plastic bag, Pope Francis didn't have enough brains to make a decent headache. Powers didn't give Protestants the time of day: "ecumenical" wasn't in his vocabulary; now and then, if invited, he'd golf with Lutheran or Methodist pastors and crush them without mercy, in silence, except for offering advice on correct stance as they teed up the ball. He had bursitis in his left shoulder and had to correct his stance for it, and to gauge the correction he wore a lead sinker hung down like a plumb bob from the bill of his cap. He'd tee up his ball, toss a pinch of grass to test the wind, get his feet dug in, adjust the plumb bob, waggle the club a couple dozen times, and take a quick off-balance swing, and hit a perfect drive that rose and rose and dropped and rolled onto the green 250 yards away, and say, "Well, not bad for an old man with a bum shoulder." But playing with a Catholic hacker with a pile of dough, he could hit a sand trap accurately and then join him in tall grass and hit multiple putts while walking with the donor and discussing Protestants and how they believe in golf with no holes, a driving range theology, just hit so it feels good.

He had little sympathy for Father Wilmer, but the Catholic laity did. How could you banish a good man who'd said one ugly thing and replace him with a priest who had no gift for small talk, who considered himself better than others, a cardinal sin in a small town? A large contingent of them opted to drive to St. Joseph for Sunday Mass or St. Rosa. The next week the Our Lady bulletin referred to "swindling membership" when surely it meant "dwindling." If not, Father Powers said, at least the swindlers had moved to another church, one friendlier to larceny. Or, in the case of Lutherans, larsony. He did not mind dwindlement. The Church is not for everyone, just as Chesterton is not or James Joyce. Golf is not for everyone. Some people are better suited to wearing a big helmet and lunging forward against other large men. The number of great Lutheran shortstops you can count on one hand with a few fingers to spare.

For Easter Mass, Our Lady congregants were surprised to see Mr. Westby, a Lutheran, who'd sold his dairy farm and moved to Florida four years before with his wife, Alma, and now here he was among Catholics. What gives? Alma was a true Lutheran, heavyset and enigmatic. Her motto was, "Never pass up the chance to keep your mouth shut." But she came alive once on a vacation in Florida, she chattered and laughed and sang and danced, so after the Mister developed back problems, he sold the farm and bought a Spanish cottage on Longboat Key with a walled swimming pool, and Alma looked at him, tears in her eyes, and said, "This is what I always wanted in life and never knew it." They bought two Pekingese, Bella and Stella, who became their grandchildren. Their daughter, Deb, was a singer called Alyssa Permission with the band Doubtful Pajamas, a girl

with shaved head and two big wings tattooed across her clav-
icle, and their son, Don, was a waiter who'd been living with
a friend named Dave for 11 years, both of them in New York.
The Westbys loved their Florida life and hardly ever left their
walled swimming pool. They were in seventh heaven. They sent
a Christmas card north with a picture of Bella and Stella wearing water wings in the pool. The dogs barked on the Westbys'
voice-mail message. The dogs sat at the table with them and ate
the same food. And then one day, while Alma left them for a
moment in the walled yard, the dogs died. Evidently, they ate
a poisonous plant, a vine that had grown into the yard through
a crack in the wall. The Westbys were devastated. They could
not bear to stay another day. They put the house up for rent
and came back to Minnesota, back to winter, back to grief. His
brother Les had died, and they moved in with his widow, Jane,
who had been depressed before and now was submerged in misery, sitting in a darkened bedroom listening to Frankie Valli,
her late husband's favorite singer. Mr. Westby asked Pastor Liz,
"How could God allow this to happen, when we were finally so
happy? I hated dairy farming. I was a convict in a prison run
by Holsteins. Florida was paradise. Our dogs were our family.
I thought God was a loving dog." Pastor Liz clearly heard him
say "loving dog" and decided not to mention it. She said, "I'm
sorry you and Alma have been so upset. I can understand how
you feel." But he didn't want to be understood, he wanted to
understand God's cruelty. So they went to Our Lady for Easter.

Alma despised Frankie Valli, and she thought they should
try Florida again and get two new dogs and learn to love them.
Mr. Westby said he could do that but wanted to spend time in

New York first, reconciling with Deb and Don. Alma said, "Let them reconcile with us, they were the ones who spit in our face, why should we make the effort?" They went to Our Lady for Easter, and Mr. Westby read the bulletin and there was a verse that burned in his brain. And he stood up and though it went against his shy retiring nature, he spoke it aloud as the organ was playing the prelude. "Love one another. As I have loved you, so you must love one another. By this all men will know that you are my disciples, if you love one another." The organ played louder and he shouted it. And people looked at each other, and they all thought, *Cheese.* Gary the town constable sat down by him and asked, "Are you all right?" "I belong to the Lord," said Mr. Westby. "Are you done shouting?" said Gary. "Yes," he said. Father Powers shook hands with him after Mass. Mr. Westby repeated the verse, "Love one another." "Good idea, you've come to the right place," said Father Powers. The Westbys were in agreement that if they heard Frankie Valli sing "Can't Take My Eyes Off of You" one more time, they'd commit violent acts, so they headed for New York and got a room in a hotel near Grand Central Station. They met their children separately for lunch at the Oyster Bar. Deb had quit singing and become Judeo-Christian and worked in a church school and asked to borrow $5,000 to have her tattoos removed. Don and Dave were working at the same Spanish restaurant and were very busy with their men's choral group and a theater company called Epic Inclinations. Each lunch lasted an hour and a half, and that was more than long enough. Mr. Westby ordered oysters and then said to the waiter, "I'm sorry but these oysters are raw." There was not much conversation, but the restaurant was packed with people so there was plenty to look at. Back at the hotel, he and Alma sat in their room, listening to a woman in the next room sobbing at a TV movie with a dog in it, and they agreed that their children were like strangers at a bus stop, there was nothing to reconcile about, and he said, "Let's go back to Florida and love each other," and so they did. Someone told me they bought two more little dogs and are quite content. I don't know, but I wouldn't be surprised. In any case, they are Lutheran no longer and probably not Catholic either. Their dogma is about the great commandment to love and also about dogs.

All unhappy marriages are alike; each happy marriage is happy in its own way and a mystery to outsiders. The phone rings and Alma answers it and she chatters to the outsider in a reasonable way, and then she hangs up, and Mr. Westby asks, "Who was it?" and she says, "Al," and he says, "Oh, how's he?" "Fine." And then they resume their own language, whose vocabulary is much smaller, and some of which is made up of silences. The beauty of it is that you don't have to say how you feel, the other person knows. Now and then there are bad feelings when the marriage is tested and they push at the walls and the walls hold. Sometimes they don't answer the phone. The call goes to voice mail, and they hear a man offer them tremendous savings on something they don't need like life insurance or a time-share in Florida, and as time goes by, there is more and more they don't need, just each other who share the language of love.

8

THERAPIST

The therapist Alice found was Ashley Allison, LMFT, which stands for "Licensed Marriage Family Therapist" but to older people was reminiscent of LSMFT, "Lucky Strike Means Fine Tobacco," which some people mentioned to her when she arrived and which didn't amuse her but she was nice about it. She arrived the Wednesday after Easter, in a car with a bumper sticker (HONK IF YOU NEED TO TALK ABOUT IT), she was 28, tall, friendly in a professional way, affirmative but not seeking a friendship, pleasantly dressed—white blouse, slacks, jacket, sandals—nothing remarkable that you'd point to with interest. She was about neutrality.

Alice took her to lunch at the Moonlight Bay supper club, opening its new season with a fish fry. Ashley ordered a Caesar salad, hold the croutons. Alice started to tell her about the cheese epidemic and the outbreaks of unseemliness, and Ashley waved her off. "I want to hear it from the grass roots," she said. "I need to avoid premature conclusions. But what end result do we have in mind? What's the goal?"

"This used to be a very friendly town. There were rifts, of course, and some old family feuds, but by and large people got along and there was a willingness to cooperate, which you really need in a little town—people who'll volunteer for Flag Day or the Halloween parade or Christmas decorations or whatever.

"For the school Prom last year, people pitched in, even those who had no kids in school, to decorate the gym and the parking lot. The theme was 'A Night in Barbados,' six truckloads of sand had to be hauled in to make the dune in the parking lot and 6,000 palm fronds had to be cut out of paper and pasted to the papier-mâché trunks and twinkling lights installed, and we went around town borrowing tables and we made sweet-and-sour pork and pineapple appetizers, a huge project, and we were just finishing up and slipping out the back door, filthy and sweaty, as our beautiful children came in through the front, all dolled up, shiny and happy. Kristina Diener was the Queen of the Prom and looked so elegant she belonged in a fashion magazine, and we knew this was the last we'd maybe ever see of her. We gave them a night to remember and never expected thanks for it and didn't get any and came home and had beans and fried Spam and waited up until 2 a.m. for the kids to come home. That's what I'm talking about.

"We need to focus on our kids and, to do that, the grownups have to avoid bickering and bad behavior. Ever since the epidemic, I see people talking mean talk, getting in a huff, avoiding each other. We don't have the ease and warmth we used to have. And if we lose that, then I have no idea who we are."

Ashley said, "I know. Trauma can be very confusing. We

all live with social façades and when they drop, it can make us feel terribly vulnerable. I thought I was lesbian for several years, and when I found out otherwise, it was disorienting. But sometimes the loss of façades can lead to more honest communication. New ways of validation. I'm just not sure it's possible to return to what existed before. Self-actualization can be a lifelong process and we don't want to get in the way of it. Trauma might very well lead to something better."

Alice's lunch came. A rather hefty cheeseburger and onion rings and a vanilla shake. Ashley was content with her salad and a glass of water. Alice pushed her basket of onion rings toward her, by way of an offering. Ashley smiled and shook her head.

"What you call a façade," Alice said, "may be what we'd consider a person's good reputation. And whatever self-actualization is, I think it's supposed to happen before you're 15, but I doubt it's going to happen to people in their 60s and 70s. A façade can be an honest façade. Good manners make good neighbors. I don't mean to be difficult, but a town has its own way of doing things that may not be according to the textbook, but it's how things work here."

Ashley had something in her teeth. She dug in her purse for dental floss.

"Let's do this," Alice said. "Let's announce that you're here for a week and you're happy to listen to people's problems and everything is confidential, and if they like, they can talk on the phone or Zoom you or whatever makes them comfortable."

Ashley said, "That's fine, but I was sort of thinking we'd work in groups so people are challenged to practice openness with those whom they need to be open with."

Alice tried to point out that openness was part of the problem here—openness in the sense of "nakedness," the postmaster singing a right-wing song on government property, for example. Pastor Liz sermonizing about herself wearing a toilet seat.

So they worked out a compromise. Ashley would listen to people's problems confidentially, one by one, and maybe there would be group therapy eventually but not yet nor anytime soon unless people wanted that.

Lenny joined them for dessert. She was recovered from her flu. It was only stomach upset, no cheese had been involved. She'd sent a sample to the lab for analysis. "I'm glad we've got science on the job," said Ashley. "When it comes to chemistry, I am clueless. I never got beyond acid and alkali." Lenny said psych was her worst subject: common sense posing as science. "I couldn't agree more," said Ashley. "Psych is an art, not a science." The two of them became instant friends. Lenny ordered a vodka sour. Alice got one too, then Ashley ordered a gin martini. Lenny said, "What the heck. My husband ran off with a folksinger. Twenty years of worrying if I was sexy enough, and a string bean with a Junior Miss bra sings 'Wimoweh' and he goes apeshit."

"Your husband is sleepwalking," said Ashley. "It happens to men in their 50s and 60s. They go into a cloud. Unbelievabubble."

Lenny said, "He wrote to me today. He wants me to meet his girlfriend. Where does this sort of stupidity come from? Did he read it on a website? Is it from a sitcom?"

"Tell him you're busy. Three words: 'Sorry. Can't. Busy.' If he calls, don't pick up."

Alice said that her husband had been an architect and decided he wanted to be a truck driver and play in a blues band, so he went and did that and found a girlfriend, and—Alice said—"It's a big relief not to be responsible for someone else's happiness. Let her deal with it. The man grew up in Winnetka, he studied with Marcel Breuer and Eero Saarinen, and now he's singing about 'hand me down my travelin' shoes, I got the Statesboro blues.' I looked up Statesboro, it's in Georgia. The man's never been to Georgia in his life. You're supposed to do this when you're 18, and the man is 67."

Lenny said she wanted to make a fresh start in life and was thinking Colorado. Minnesota was too flat, too much sameness, she wanted to be near mountains, for the mystery of them. The three debated having another drink and decided not to and then said, "Why not?" and had a shot of brandy apiece, Alice's treat. Lenny said that today was the happiest she'd been in three years. "Who needs cheese when you have friends?" she said. "If you depend on cheese to break through your inhibitions, then what's it all about?" It was excellent brandy. She'd grown up the smartest girl in school and was six feet tall by the time she hit puberty, so boys avoided her, and she didn't bother to repress her intelligence around them. She joined 4-H and pledged her head to clearer thinking, her heart to greater loyalty, her hands to larger service, her health to better living, and she stuck with the pledge even as other kids pledged themselves to superstition, hormonal anger, social media, and musical stupidity. She won the Shining Star scholarship in 12th grade and, over her parents' opposition, went to Athena College instead of St. Olaf and fell in among Unitarians and took to it instantly—all the magical tricks of virgin birth and resurrection replaced by rational free-thinking.

Athena College was the first to have open dorms, no restrictions, the first to eliminate the study of colonialist literature and to use non-rectangular unlined writing paper, and every year on May Day the students run naked through the campus with streamers to entwine around the Maypole. They were the first college in America to have an all-lesbian women of color Department of Physics, the first to have a transgender president and not a single white male on the Board of Trustees. She majored in philosophy but was in over her head, and the next spring she switched to biology. She got her epidemiology degree from the University of Minnesota, hoping to serve humanity by fighting disease, and she gave it her best shot, but what she found is that science exists in a bureaucratic cellblock in which the dullards rise to the top and those who love the science labor in the cellar late into the night and then butt heads with politics. In other words, argue with arrogant people who are also stupid. She was struggling in her job, and then Greg sprang his surprise and she had a breakdown. She tried to get out of bed one morning and couldn't. She felt as if she weighed a thousand pounds. She thought of going to a mental hospital, but her insurance policy didn't cover it. And then her mother called and told her about Liz and Clint and the outbursts of nuttiness in town and the dam broke, and Lenny sobbed into the phone and felt better and drove up from Dallas and now she was ready to begin a new life. Ashley leaned over and hugged her for a long time.

They finished the drinks and Alice paid the tab, and they joined arms and walked out into the sunshine and looked at the lake and the roofs of town across the water. "One thing about living in a small town," Alice said, "you do get to know people up close and personal. Of course, it helps if you're a woman. Men sit in a fish house and look at a hole in the ice and listen to the radio. Women, you catch them at the right time when they're in the mood, they'll talk till the cows come home. Every woman I know contains a whole book and if you say the right word you'll get a whole chapter or two. Two women and two telephones, you might get *The Odyssey* and *The Iliad*."

9

TRUE STORIES

Alice wanted to suppress the cheese and Lenny was curious about the science and Ashley wanted to practice her therapy skills and the cheeseheads wanted a chance to exercise righteous anger, and meanwhile the *Herald Star* ignored the whole thing, not wanting to offend or annoy, and I decided that what my town needed was a good book. There is something awe-inspiring in the loss of inhibition. I keep wanting to lose mine and then I look over the edge and it scares me. I want to write in honor of my dead, my old aunts, old teachers like Fern and Bertha and Helen, classmates who are gone, Corinne and Leeds and Roger. I love my town, my fellow Christians who hold hands and pray over the hotdish, the teenagers striving for cool, the old men who sit in the Sidetrack and hope to live to be 90 and enjoy their whiskey and have all their marbles to the very end and die in bed, perhaps shot cleanly by a jealous husband. When one of them dies, the others raise their glasses and say, "That's one less here, and one more there, and now there's more fish for the rest of us." And now they're all gone. All the old men who looked at me with grave suspicion are gone. Nobody is left to warn us not to think we're so smart. The only old men left are my classmates, and we're all in the same boat, and it's sinking.

The Wobegon I knew slipped away like a ship in the night. I missed Darlene at the counter of the Chatterbox. If you should mention Father Emil in passing or the Thanatopsis Society or the Sons of Knute, she knew what you were talking about, and that gave the conversation some breadth and depth. Darlene's daughter Cathy, who took over waitressing, has no interest in history, only in her personal story, the slights she's suffered, the unfairness of life, her victimization at the hands of enemies. I'm afraid she gets up in the morning with no gladness, no thanksgiving. Lord, have mercy.

I am not ashamed of creating fiction. I once (true story) was asked to give the elegy at my classmate Bert's memorial service in Minneapolis in 2012. I said yes, though I didn't know Bert, but neither did anyone else. He and Elise split up after 10 years, and she remarried and moved to Chicago with the kids and Bert stayed in Minneapolis, a cashier at Walmart. He kept to himself, came to one reunion and I asked him what he was up to and he said he was collecting bus transfers. He had transfers from all 50 states, Canada and Mexico, Puerto Rico, and 60 other countries, more than 6,000 slips of paper in all. The next Bus Collectors convention would be in Montreal and he planned to go. He hoped to sell his collection and invest the money in expanding his collection of 741 alarm clocks to 1,440 so he could have a 24-hour ring-off, an alarm sounding every minute for 24 hours. He never made it. He died a month before Montreal. Elise asked me to clear out his apartment. I took his lifetime collection of bus transfers out to the incinerator and burned them so as to make other collections more valuable. Life belongs to the living.

I went to the funeral chapel and, after a rental minister gave a generic funeral sermon about the corruptible putting on the incorruptible, I felt I owed it to Bert to give him a boost. I stood up next to the little urn of ashes and looked out at the 16 mourners, and I said, "Bert was a loner, as we all know, and few people knew that he spoke Cantonese, a difficult language with nine key tones, almost indistinguishable to the Western ear, which he learned for his few Chinese customers. He found his true self in Cantonese, which sometimes happens with learning a foreign tongue. He loved the Cantonese saying, 'Your home is gone and you'll never find it and the destination you're headed for is an illusion and the place where you are is unbearable and you have to escape from it.' He wrote a song, "Bus Transfer Blues" and I sang it to them.

I've been riding this bus long enough,
Going to transfer to another.
Take a bus back home,
See my father and my mother.
We're all passengers on a bus
And there's one thing I know.
We've got to transfer to get there
Where we were meant to go.

I wanted them to believe he had a rich inner life and they were glad to believe it, especially his kids were. They were moved to tears. I gave them a good memory. Maybe he suffered from lifelong depression but that's his business, no reason his kids should grieve about it. It wasn't the first dishonest eulogy ever given.

But the best stories are ones that are true, or mostly, and that's the reason to go back home. I turned off my phone, sat with a cup of coffee and a crossword puzzle, and when someone approached, I smiled and offered them a chair. "Beautiful day out there," I said. "You're looking pretty sharp today." And eventually they told me what they needed to tell me. If you offer an amiable silence, people will talk.

Dorothy had found a boyfriend, a tall order at 73. His name was Vern, he was from Willmar, she met him at a church supper, he whipped potatoes for her and didn't drown them in butter. They conversed and she heard some grammar problems, *lay* instead of *lie* and and "warsh" for "wash," but she could deal with that. His wife died a year ago, she was "laying," actually *lying*, in the yard when she had a heart attack and was gone. Dorothy's husband Arnold ran off 20 years ago with a waitress, that old story. She and Vern found that they both love to dance, both walk at the same brisk pace, both like neatness, both want to travel to interesting places, Tibet, the Arctic, New Zealand. She said, "I wake up in the morning thinking I'd like go back to sleep, but I know that getting up makes me feel better so I do, I get busy, I feel great." He said, "I'm the same. I don't like to lay around. Get up, get warshed, get going." He isn't a fisherman, doesn't care about football, doesn't like fast food. He sounded perfect. They sort of fell in love, as old people do, tentatively, trying not to think about what went wrong the last time. But people could tell it was love. Women in love look the way Botticelli painted them. Men in love look like someone bonked them with a baseball bat. They were both in love. And then one day, out of nowhere, he launched into a diatribe about vaccination being a vehicle for biological warfare waged by Unitarians and how M.D.s are in cahoots with it and this is the reason why kids can't do math, and she listened, stupefied. She'd found the perfect man and he was a moron. He listened to the radio in his sleep over tiny earbuds and obviously, he was tuned to the station for the stupid. She looked up his Facebook page, which was full of links to articles proving that global warming is a hoax cooked up by old hippies. Why hadn't she looked at it before? Why had she wasted two months on him? To hell with him. She handed him his pajamas and sent him back to Willmar. But she missed him, even with his craziness. She had deleted his number from her phone but she still had it in her head. "Should I call him?" she said. I told her to let sleeping dogs lay. She knew I was right but she didn't like it. I could hear her thinking: *I'm 73 and that man was my last lover. There won't be another.* Me and her are in the same boat except my last lover is still married to me and if she adopted crazy ideas like your hair should be warshed only every other day, I would try hard to go along with it.

I sat like a mouse in the corner as the Lutheran women met to discuss the annual Sweethearts Dance, and Claudia Johnson stood up and said, "I may be in the minority but I feel strongly that the polka is a form of foreplay and the only purpose is seduction and to get into the back seat of a car and unzip your pants and have sex. And I include ballet in that, too: the display of bare legs is sexual, no doubt about it. But the polka is worse because the couple grabs hold of each other and the beat gives

you the impulse to hop and twirl and it's a rehearsal for intercourse. Marching band is different and drill team, but when you
put on a dance, you are issuing an open invitation for people to
enter into unwise relationships. I know something about this.
When I was in 4-H, Byron Tollefson invited me to the Future
Farmers dance and I went, I was 14, and he had his hands all
over me and he tried to get me to go for a walk in the woods and
it wasn't to look at the trees, it was more about the birds and the
bees, so I said no, and we went back to the gym and they were
playing "Beer Barrel Polka" and he kept spinning me so his arm
would brush against my bosom and I told him to stop, and four
months later Kathy, who'd been out with him once, quit school
because she was pregnant. No, you should consider the girls
you're putting into a very vulnerable position."

There was silence. The woman was valedictorian of her grad-
uating class, a history major at Hamline. Then I remembered:
Claudia was a Scheidecker before she was a Johnson and the
Scheideckers sat by Earl and Myrna at Sunday morning Breaking of Bread. Claudia grew up Brethren like me and not even a
Hamline education could erase it. All it took was some cheese to
bring it out. Virginia Ingqvist thanked her for her opinion and
called for a report from the Refreshment Committee.

I sat in the back row of the Men's Fellowship gathering and
Ray Holmberg gave a little talk about how we should thank the
Lord for every day we walk this earth, and then he talked about
his brother Rex, asking us to keep Rex in our prayers. Rex had
been the high school janitor. He tried to be a good person but
didn't feel good about it so he tried experimenting with sins,
starting with sloth, which came to him naturally, and then, for

gluttony, he ate two pepperoni pizzas every night and a half gallon of vanilla ice cream with hot fudge, then moved on to lust and found a website where women post nude photos of themselves. He spent a few weeks there, and said, "When you've looked at thousands of nude women, they start to all look alike." So he did greed and sought ecstasy in mushrooms that gave him the sensation of lightness and being covered with feathers. After that, anger didn't interest him, or pride, and then his uncle Oscar in Chicago died and left him a hundred grand and he met a woman named Melissa, a former Miss Iowa, and fell in love with her, so that took care of envy.

He exhausted the vices and he and Melissa settled in Des Moines and opened an art gallery where your doctor's sonogram of your beating heart, set to a Schubert "Sanctus," becomes a video installation mounted in a frame you can hang on the wall that is activated by Alexa when you say the words, "Oh, my God." Rex had been a janitor and played second base for the Whippets, weak bat, good glove, and now he lives with a beauty queen and is in the video art business.

Someone said, "What is the point of the story? What is the lesson here?" They looked at me because I am the oldest. I quoted Pythagoras. "The shortest distance is not always a straight line." It's all I remember from high school geometry. I've used this quotation dozens of times in meetings involving more than seven persons, discussing things I don't understand at all, and it has always impressed people.

Tibby Marklund, the organist at Lake Wobegon Lutheran, sat down at my table and with no preface said, "I heard you talking about memory—I had an experience when my father-in-law was dying of pancreatic cancer and I sat at his bedside and held his hand. His wife couldn't deal with it, and my husband was working on a pipeline project up north. Johnny was so sick and he slept a lot and only ate ice cream. It seemed odd to me that, at the end of your life, so little time left, you'd want to sleep all the time. When I first met the family, I said to them, 'I don't know if Harvey told you but I'm Jewish,' and his mom said, 'Oh, that's fine, dear. We're so glad we got the chance to meet you.' As if this might be the end of it. But it wasn't. I married my Swede because I loved him and saw the faithfulness and honesty of him and I valued that more than style. Good father, sweet husband, the same from week to week. You didn't go to bed with Mark Twain and wake up with the Marquis de Sade. The day before Johnny died, he looked at me and thanked me, and he said, 'That's enough, I had a good life. I'm ready to go.' And in the morning, he was dead. I washed his face and combed his hair and folded his hands, and out of the depths of my memory, I don't know where it came from, but I prayed the prayer I'd memorized for my grandmother ages ago. Suddenly it was sitting there in my head and I chanted it as I had heard it as a child. *Yisgadal v'yiskadash sh'mei raba . . . Exalted and hallowed be God's great name in the world which God created, according to plan. May God's majesty be revealed in the days of our lifetime and the life of all Israel—speedily, imminently, to which we say: Amen. Blessed be God's great name to all eternity. Blessed, praised, exalted, glorified, and adored, be the name of the Holy Blessed One, beyond all earthly words and songs of blessing, praise, and comfort. To which we say: Amen.* It was still there in my head. I'd said it for Grandma Tottie, from the North Side of Minneapolis, a proud member of Mikro Kodesh Synagogue, who grew up in Yiddish, and who was proud to be Russian Jewish, not German. She was Mrs. Fields, though originally they'd been Feldmans, and if people inquired about her ancestry, she said, 'We were Feldman. Not the Finkelstein Fields, the Feldman Fields.' And so I said Kaddish for an old Swede. His wife was at exercise class, his son was laying pipe, his other son was a shrink in Denver, and a Jew had given thanks to the Holy Blessed One in his name. That's what happened."

I put my hand on her hand on the table and she put her other hand on mine and I put a hand on top and I said, "As you have given, may it be given to you, joy and abundance of life, and the Lord God make his face to shine upon you and be gracious unto you, all the days of your life. Amen." "And also with you," she said.

Two days later, Lenny dashed into the cafe out of breath looking for Alice and heard her voice and turned, and her bag bounced off Clarence who was starting to sip a cup of hot coffee and some of it dribbled down him so she had to stop and apologize and mop it up—Louise at the lab had called and said they found the virus, a passive pathogen with a CNA protein exhibiting variable phenotypes whose plasticity is related to its toxicity. In other words, the same virus might cause angry outbursts in some and inappropriate affections in another and irrational lectures in someone else. Due to the properties peculiar to the composite protons, mixed-effects models are the rule rather than the exception. The mutation is accelerated by the adulteration of the letcons. Epidemiologists thought the virus had been eradicated but it reappeared, carried by Canadian tortoises who regurgitate their prey and save it in their nests for winter, including tree toads who are susceptible to the virus, and some toads escaped and were eaten by whooping cranes and the virus was spread in their droppings as they migrated south, and due to a mild winter traces of the virus survived in thistles, that were eaten by Hilmar's reindeer. "We have to report this to the State Health Board," Louise said. "They may need to inspect the farm and confiscate the cheese."

Lenny told her, "Tell the health people that it comes from a Norwegian bachelor farmer who is paranoid about government agents and who is well-armed, so before they accost him personally they should organize a posse of his friends and relations."

Louise said the virus affects people's brains differently, but the common result is temporary loss of social filter.

"I know," Lenny said. "We've been seeing a lot of that lately."

Alice thought they should talk to Dr. DeHaven, so they did. He listened to Lenny's summary of the lab report and said, "These people are epidemiologists, they see trouble wherever they look. If it were up to them, everybody'd be locked in their homes and wearing surgical masks. It's an epidemic of ignorance is what it is. A bunch of schoolgirls getting sympathetic illness."

Lenny leaned in and gave him a good look. "You look jaundiced to me," she said.

"People have been telling me that for years," he said.

10

JOHNNY ROGERS

Roger Hedlund was on the trail of Roger Johnson, aka Johnny Rogers, born in Lake Wobegon in 1953, remembered by a few people as a sad kid with no friends who got in trouble for shoplifting and graduated in 1971 without having distinguished himself in anything. None of his classmates had a clear memory of him except that he liked to collect June bugs and clip their wings and drop them in girls' dresses. He was sent to the school for the dim-witted and disappeared. The family moved away in 1972. His dad was married to Lois Ingqvist, a second cousin once removed of Hjalmar and Virginia. Nobody noticed when he changed his name to Johnny Rogers and became a country music star. He wore his hair in a mullet, and he tried to be an outlaw, though he'd started out singing a sweet sad song that probably was about Lake Wobegon—

Birches and a big elm tree,
On a porch just you and me.
Tulips all thick and sweet,

Lonely neighbors on the street.
The whistle of a southbound train,
Summer night, feels like rain.

The folks and I don't belong.
Nobody knows us in this town.
Nobody needs us, that is clear.
So where do we go from here?
Crickets murmur in the grass
The trains go through and the hours pass.

It was sweet, two acoustic guitars and bass and drums, but it came out at the wrong time, when Nashville was deep into testosterone, and the album went straight to the remainder bins and Johnny wound up touring in a Winnebago as part of a package show with a *Hee Haw* comedian, a gospel quartet, and a girl singer with big hair named Loretta Betts who gave him gonorrhea. It was humiliating.

As Lucky Luciano once said, "If you find yourself eating dirt, it is good to stop right away, else you may come to develop a liking for it," and Johnny Rogers went into the studio with a pedal steel, drums, electric guitar, and changed his sound, hitting the low notes:

You look at me like I was giving off an odor,
You got your daughter in the car and started up the motor
And you closed the windows and locked up the doors
And I thought to myself: Up yours.

The album was *Proud of Who I Am*, and it produced a No.1 hit, his first.

> *My beer's gone flat and I lost my hat and I'm getting fat, she tells me.*
> *It's all that steak 'n' burgers with bacon that's makin' this great big belly.*
> *An' I walk with a gimp and I feel like a simp and my willie's gone limp and I'm stuck in*
> *A lower gear and I'm out of beer but I'm here so I'll keep on truckin'.*

None of this made an impression in Lake Wobegon. He was an unknown there, but his manager rented the school auditorium to record a concert album, *Coming Home,* in 1997. Ticket sales were slim, there being no fans in town, so they had to bus in an audience, and the day before, Johnny came back and did a video of himself walking by his old house on Taft Street and he got so depressed thinking about his boyhood, looking at the little basement window where he spent hours trying to make a G7th chord, he went in his trailer and downed a pint of Jim Beam sprinkled with fentanyl and became comatose and had to be flown to a hospital. The concert was canceled. He wasn't a big enough star for his collapse to make the news. A plane landed at the St. Cloud airport and he was loaded in and hardly anyone was aware of it. The album was recorded in Nashville with prerecorded applause, and it reached No. 189 on the charts and stalled there. It was the beginning of the end. He did another outlaw album, *I'm The Man That Peterbilt*, but that wave was at ebb and then he did an album of pop standards that was universally mocked for his growly "Somewhere Over the Rainbow" and then he did *Get Your Hands Off My Flag* with the single "Find Your Own Nation"—

You liberals and this lousy life you're leadin',
I think you'd be happier in Sweden.
Or maybe in France
Where the women wear the pants.

But Johnny was in no shape to tour in behalf of the album. He appeared as an opening act to Donald J. Trump at some speeches in 2013 and 2014 but was unsteady with the lyrics and had a hard time playing rhythm guitar, and was dropped by Mr. Trump's organization and left behind in Las Vegas, where he got drunk and lost his billfold and his cell phone ran out of power and in desperation he went out on the highway to hitch a ride and—Irony Alert—it was a foggy night and he was standing by an exit ramp and he was struck and killed by a semi hauling a load of fresh horse manure to an organic tea plantation in Arizona. It made the news, and a posthumous album, *Live a Trucker, Die a Trucker*, sold well, and Mr. Dixon, who'd been a big fan, made it his mission to keep Johnny's legacy alive by establishing a trucker park in Lake Wobegon where anybody could get behind the wheel of a Peterbilt and drive it around a track. Johnny had never driven a truck himself, but now anybody who wanted could take a turn at the wheel. It'd be the only park like it in the country, a patriotic playground, every day would be the Fourth of July. You could put on the virtual reality headgear and be a drum major leading the Marine Corps band, or wade ashore at Normandy or raise the flag at Iwo Jima, or stand in front of a vast crowd and say whatever you like and when you touch the *Applause* pad they will clap and when you touch *Standing O* they will rise and cheer and do your heart a world of good.

11

GLORIOUS SPRING

It was spring, glorious spring, daffodils, tulips, crocuses, butterflies floating on the breeze, and the fragrance of hay and alfalfa in the air, loons calling across the lake. Mr. Bjornson led his and Mrs. Nelson's biology classes on a long hike—she was pregnant and feeling nauseous—and he was excited as usual by the abundance of life, hummingbirds, grasshoppers, mother porcupine and her baby living in an abandoned woodchuck burrow under a pile of brush, robins mating and bluebirds, barn swallows newly arrived from Argentina, sitting on the telephone lines, waiting to make their nests of mud and straw, the males hauling the mud, the females supervising the design, turtles sunning themselves on the rocks, and then he heard the boys bringing up the rear, gossiping, laughing, and he turned and said, "Why do I bother? What's the point? Some of you have less curiosity than the average barn swallow, and all you do is get in the way of the few who want to learn—you think you're cool but you're mainly just dull, and your dullness probably means that you'll get bored with marriage and your kids and your job as well, and you'll seek out chemical roads to deeper and darker dullness, and you'll die of boredom without ever having learned a goddamn thing, and I wish I could help you but you're beyond help and, though it's not nice to say it, the world would be better off if you got shit-faced Friday night and drove your car at high speed with the headlights off and ran into a bridge abutment. Considering the fact that you'll never amount to anything, it would be a patriotic deed on your part. Save society's resources for those who would make use of them. That's how it works in nature. The lazy barn swallows are picked off by the hawks and everybody's better for it. The men I knew who died in Iraq had a lot to contribute to their country, and maybe you should've died in their place and if you'd been in their place, we would've lost the war a lot sooner and saved the country trillions of dollars. So there's the irony. Now, if you look straight ahead at that fence post you'll see a meadowlark and now you hear its distinctive song, the purpose of which is to attract a mate and to warn away competitors. He is giving it all he's got. The puzzle is: why did God create the indifferent? That's what I don't understand."

He was reported to Mr. Halvorson for the use of the word "shit-faced," and was called to the office and given a talking-to about there being no hopeless cases and the possibility of students learning while showing no signs of it and how it's not helpful to suggest that students kill themselves by driving dangerously. Mr. Halvorson recognized teaching fatigue and forgave it, especially in the case of an excellent teacher like Mr. Bjornson. He did inquire about cheese usage, and Mr. Bjornson said he only used Parmesan and only on cooked food. Except for some at the Nelsons' house. "Local cheese? Soft and sort of grayish? Rather strong?" Mr. Bjornson nodded. Mr. Halvorson recommended that he stay away from it in the future. He said, "Something similar happened to us last fall. My wife makes sauerkraut that she puts in a crock and we bury it in the backyard with big stones on top because it ferments and sometimes it has exploded, but taken in moderation, it does have the power to clear the mind. But last fall, we had a little too much and we said, 'Alexa, play *Le Sacre du Printemps*' and she played 'Honky Tonk Women' and we danced and it frightened the children."

Mr. Bjornson asked if cheese was involved. Mr. Halvorson said no, only sauerkraut.

May 1st was Senator K. Thorvaldson's 100th birthday, though he didn't seem fully aware of it, so his daughter Mary decided against a big party for fear the crowd would excite him and he'd do his epic Lindbergh, Babe Ruth, ice-cutting, and tornado stories all at once, maybe mingle them into one. Instead, she took him to lunch with three old friends, two of whom he recognized, and she brought up the delicate subject of his '96 Buick, which he is still driving though it's big as a barge and he can barely see over the dashboard, but still he drives with great confidence. She mentioned selling it and he said, "Why? It still runs good." She said, "Anyplace you need to go, I can take you." The old man said, "There may be places I want to go that I don't want you to know about." He's half-senile but still has a sense of humor.

Mary had her dad's urologist implant a little transmitter in his groin, and now she can keep track of him on her cell phone with her Locator App. She had to go fetch him once when he dropped in at a retirement dinner and thought he was the honoree. Once he slipped into the announcer's booth at the ballpark, and when the crowd sang the national anthem, he sang, "When the red red robin comes bob-bob-bobbin' along." The only drawback is that when he scratches himself, on her phone it sounds like he is being torn from limb to limb. And if someone turns on a microwave nearby, the old man gets very happy and tries to dance with any woman within reach. This happened at the birthday lunch. Someone ordered a bowl of soup, and suddenly Senator K. jumped up and grabbed Myrtle Krebsbach and twirled her around and she was rather pleased and brushed against his crotch and felt the transmitter and said, "Boy, if you said the word, we could get married." Florian was right there and he said, "I want to be the best man." She said, "You haven't been the best man for 25 years, why start now?"

And then Senator K. got a look in his eye and said, "You wouldn't remember it, but back in 1933 the Gibb Sisters spent a winter in town living with their aunt, a Mrs. Pendleton, who was a teacher. Third grade. Later she taught fourth, but that year she taught third. The Gibb Sisters were what they used to call Siamese twins traveling with the Barnum & Bailey Circus, and their railroad car broke down in North Dakota and they had to make their way via touring car and Mrs. Pendleton was the closest relative so they spent three months with her. Mary and Margaret Gibb. They were joined at the back of the hip and I became friends with Margaret who loved to dance and I think she was attracted to me, and Mary liked to play the accordion and Margaret and I would dance and it was very romantic. Odd, of course, but you get used to it, especially with a pretty woman involved."

His daughter Mary and the others listened in amazement. This was the first time they'd heard this story. At the age of 100, the old man had finally remembered something new.

"Margaret was the dancer but it was Mary who fell in love with me, and we'd sit on the porch and Margaret pretended to doze off and then we kissed and snuggled and Mary confessed that she wanted to be an individual, not a twin, but Margaret was terrified of separation. Surgeons had studied it and decided that since they shared the same circulatory system, one of them was apt to die and they couldn't predict which one would. Margaret was for Hoover and Mary was for Roosevelt, but they were both Presbyterian and very close, of course, knew each other's minds inside and out. Mary wanted to have a family, Margaret wanted to go to college. As I say, I was in love with Mary, but it became clear that they were joined emotionally as well as physically and that both of them were in love with me, though Margaret kept her feelings concealed until one day when we thought she was sleeping and I unbuttoned Mary's blouse and it made Margaret jealous and she reached over and slapped her sister and Mary slapped her back. I tried to separate them but of course I couldn't. Mrs. Pendleton came out and saw what had happened and sent me home, and I didn't see the two of them until the party the night before the day they left town. Mary gave Margaret a pill and Mary and I made love, which was awkward with Margaret dozy but still watching. The next day they got in a car to catch the train back to Massachusetts. They did a few more tours in fairs and freak shows, singing duets, climbing stairs, letting people touch their backs where they were joined, and then they retired. When you lose the woman you love like I did, you never forget her, and so I never married. There was nobody for me like Mary Gibb."

There was a moment of silence and then his daughter asked, "Never married? What do you mean?" pointing to herself.

"You were an accident," he said. "At the farewell party, I was making love to who I thought was Mary but it was Margaret. Nine months later, you were born in Prague and suddenly the Gibbs' act tripled in value. You were the first child born to a con-joined woman, and you and your mother and your aunt moved up to become headliners in vaudeville and royalty came to see you and there were songs written—"A Man Has Plenty to Do When He Loves Two" and "Three Hearts, Six Hands"—well, I didn't care to have a child of mine exhibited as a freak. I wanted you to have a happy normal life. So I brought a custody suit, but they stayed in Europe and kept on the move and it was hard to find a court to accept jurisdiction. But then they got tired of show business, and being the mother of a small child involved a lot of bending, which was hard on their conjoined hip, and one day my sister Kandi went out to their home in Bedford, Mass, and they turned you over to my custody. And here you are."

"Kandi? You mean my mother? The woman I thought was my mother?"

"She was your aunt. I know, it seems strange, doesn't it? But she was adopted. They named her Kandiyohi because she was abandoned by her family in the train depot in Kandiyohi and they wanted her to know where she came from in case she needed to look her people up."

He said he'd kept the story hush-hush because he didn't want to make Mary feel peculiar, but now at the age of 100, he decided to come clean. "All the people who'd be scandalized are dead now," he said. "One advantage of living so long. I forget what the other one is."

She said, "Daddy, have you been eating cheese?" He said he had not, and Mary looked through the files of the *Herald Star* in 1933 and found a picture of the Gibb sisters on the front page and she could see her resemblance to Margaret, so there it was, an awful lot to learn about yourself in just a few minutes, but Mary is a strong woman. And everyone has to come from somewhere and we just have to make the best of it, whatever it is. She was the daughter of a vaudeville star and a 100-year-old man who is excited by microwave and wants to dance with anyone available. So live with it and be your own person, sing your song, cherish your friends, be happy.

12

ALICE VS. ME

I was still pretending to work for the beatification of Sister Arvonne but was secretly working on this book, though secrecy isn't easy in a small town. I've been away too long, I don't fit in anymore (if I ever did), I wear the wrong clothes, I know nothing about cars or carpentry or gardening or child care or anything else that's useful to know, but I hung around the Chatterbox and the Sidetrack, listening for viral outbursts. I am a highly skilled listener. At the Lutheran coffee hour the Sunday before the May 9th fishing opener, Marilyn Tollerud brought out a fresh pot of coffee and dinged on it and said, "I've never said this before, but it is the height of idiocy for people to spend thousands of dollars on a boat and fishing gear and bait and gas and license and go out and spend hours casting expensive lures in the hopes of catching sunfish and crappies and northerns and walleye, the worst eating fish in the world, when for a fraction of the money you could buy a salmon or tuna steak and grill it five minutes on one side, three on the other, and have something worth eating. And in the fall, you go and chase after partridge and grouse, gimpy little birds that are to chickens as franks are to filet mignon. My dad did it, my uncles, my husband, and it's never been explained to me. So what comes next? Muskrat hunts? Owls? Why not buy SCUBA gear and wet suits and dig down where the turtles hibernate and bring them home and we women'll bust up the shells and carve out the meat for turtle stew? They say it tastes like frog legs. Maybe you could catch some bullfrogs too so we can compare."

Her husband, Daryl, looked at Clint and Clint looked at Roger and nobody spoke up. There is no mystery about it. The reason men fish and hunt is because women don't. They married women who possess powerful corrective impulses and rush to clean up things before they're spilled, to straighten and adjust, set things right. Women will edit your sentences as you speak them, and if you pause, she will finish the sentence for you. God bless her for improving your life, but it can be exhausting and so you take up fishing in order to be free of supervision.

Clarence was a fisherman at one time, and then discovered he could achieve the same purpose—serenity—without putting a hook on the line, but the rod and reel still needed to be in his hand, or nearby, otherwise he looks like he has no reason to be out in a boat.

I was writing this down on a notepad when Alice saw me and walked over and warned me not to use real names and could I please change the name of the town from Wobegon to Maplebrook. She said, "You were brought up here, and I assume you were taught manners but it isn't so apparent, frankly. I lived in St. Paul before I moved up here and I worked in Candyland and you'd walk in and say, 'A quart box of popcorn, open, with butter'—no 'please' or 'thank you,' and I'd fill up the box and did you leave a tip? No, you didn't. Every week: popcorn, jelly beans, and licorice, and never a word of thanks. And then I saw you one night on the Letterman show and it was disgusting. I still have the video. I'll send it to you. What's your e-mail?"

I told her and she sent it, and I watched it and it was painful. I was 40 or so, bearded, white suit, and I gave off a strong aura of superiority. I stood on the stage and said: "I grew up in a small town on the prairie. It wasn't the end of the world, but you could see it from there. Everyone was Lutheran, even the atheists. It was a Lutheran God they didn't believe in. We were modest people and proud of it—if you'd given us a gold trophy, we would've had it bronzed. The men had very small active vocabularies: 'Yessir' and 'Quite the deal then' and 'Boy, you just never know'—that was about it."

"Welcome back to the end of the world," she said. "Yessir. Quite the deal then." I could understand how it offended her—a Minnesota guy making fun of his people in front of a New York crowd—I get that, but it was a *long time ago*, for heaven's sake. Water over the dam and under the bridge. Get over it.

I smiled at her benignly. It is never a good idea to insult a writer who is in the midst of writing a book. He has time to get a good bead on you. *She shook her fist and the fat on her upper arm jiggled, a massive bag of adiposity. Alice isn't beautiful enough to be as dense as she is. I look at her with indifference bordering on disbelief. I can't forget the first time she and I met, but I keep trying. If my horse had a face like hers, I'd paint eyes and a mouth on his ass and teach him to walk backwards.* She looked over my shoulder, and read what I wrote, and said, "I wouldn't call you an asshole: you don't have the warmth or the depth. You're just a mistake. I look at you and think, 'The diaphragm was so tight that conception didn't occur until the next-to-last sperm.' When you shake your head, I can hear the two extra chromosomes rattle."

"Very funny," I said.

"I dare you to put it in your book," she said.

"Why? Nobody would think you said it. They'd think I made it up. They'd think it was postmodernism."

She laughed. "You? Postnasal maybe. But if they did think it was postmodernism—what do you call it? Metafiction. It'd impress your reviewers in Idaho and Wyoming."

I confessed I didn't remember what metafiction means.

She said, "I can explain it to you, but I can't understand it for you. But it might be good for your reputation. I never thought you were particularly funny."

I said, "You never thought—that was your problem."

I looked down at what I'd written about her and felt ashamed, it was so cheap and trashy, but she was wrong about me. I love where I'm from, I'm loyal to my hometown. I went off to live my own life, which took me to some high spots and bright lights, but I'm a hard worker, not a playboy. I never did drugs, never hung out with thugs, never took shortcuts, never set out to do harm. Never owned a gun, never gambled for money. The only time I went into a casino was to use the men's room. It was dark inside, hundreds of slot machines dinging and flashing and buzzing, and the men's room was way in back and hard to find, and I saw an old woman in silver slacks, bright red lipstick, a credit card on a lanyard, which she stuck in the slot machine—it was Miss Sayre, my old seventh-grade English teacher, playing the Jack O' Diamonds machine and smoking a Camel Light with an oxygen tank on her back and a tube up her nose. She was a beloved teacher of mine, who introduced me to Robert Frost and *Our Town* and John Steinbeck and *Giants in the Earth*. This woman taught me to love American literature. I approached her and I could smell the gin. She looked up and said, "I'm on this machine. Find your own machine, buster."

"Miss Sayre? I'm Gary Keillor. I was in your English class."

"A lot of people were in my English class, and I've been trying to forget them. And guess what? In your case, I succeeded."

"I really liked your English class."

"Well, at least one of us was happy then."

"Can I buy you lunch?"

"You can if you let me eat it alone."

"Is there anything else I can do for you?"

"Just go away."

It was a shock, of course, but I've come to terms with it. I still love *Our Town*, and Miss Sayre had moved on to Damon Runyon and Raymond Chandler. I still hear Emily Webb say, "Oh, earth, you're too wonderful for anybody to realize you." Miss Sayre moved on to the world of bookies and burlesque queens, horse-players, lounge pianists, nightclub bouncers, drug dealers, ladies of the night, everybody looking for the lucky draw, the inside straight, the big payoff.

She was proof that stories are real and can lead you down a road to unexpected destinations. A girl can be corrupted by a book and so can a boy. Miss Sayre was proof of it. My mother was right—it can be dangerous to read Hemingway and she begged me not to and to read the book of Luke instead, but that has its pitfalls too—"Sell all that you have and give to the poor and follow me and you shall have treasure in heaven"?? What is that all about?

I wanted to talk to Ashley. I'd seen her with Daryl and Marilyn Tollerud and Mr. Sjostrom and other people, one-on-one, always after dark and in a car with the therapee driving, the therapist in the passenger seat listening. She had figured out that Lake Wobegon people won't confide in a stranger face-to-face in a room in bright light, but at night in a car in motion, at the wheel, looking ahead down the road, they are able to open their hearts considerably. I asked a dozen people what it was she said to them and they said, "We promised not to talk about it," so finally I had to request therapy myself. I told her I need help, that I feel like a stranger in my hometown, my life feels fragile, my reputation is a spiderweb, life itself is transitory, and the next night I was driving around with Ashley, who asked what made me feel alien.

I said that I'm in the midst of writing a memoir and I'm having a problem with humility. Excessive humility. As the Norwegians say, *Du skal ikke tror at du er noget.* "Don't think you're somebody." Don't think you're special, don't think you're smart, you're not, you're no different from any of the others. This was baked into me by the time I was 10. I was brought up to be self-mortifying and take a back seat, but if I'm not special, then why am I writing about myself?

"And this is a memoir of who?" she said.

"Me."

She looked puzzled. "You?"

I told her that I used to do a radio show, called *A Prairie Home Companion.*

"Local show?"

"It started out local but then it got bigger."

"Oh," she said. She was very nice about it, she simply had never heard of me or my show, so I took her around to the library and asked Grace if she had any CDs of the show or any of my books.

"We used to," she said. "I haven't seen any in a long time. Let me look in the basement."

"Was it a call-in show?" Ashley said. No, I explained, it was a variety show, with musicians and comedy sketches and a monologue and commercials for coffee and rhubarb pie and biscuits and so forth."

"And people listened to this?"

"Yes," I said. "Quite a few people. Hundreds." I didn't feel like saying more. Time moves on. The sand castles melt in the rain. Doing a radio show is like making angels in the snow, fun at the time, but don't expect to win a prize for it.

I didn't want to embarrass Grace, who clearly had not bothered to stock my stuff in the library, so I headed up the street and Ashley walked along.

I said, "I'm working on this memoir and I came here to check my memory of events. I suffered from three bullies, terrible cruel boys who picked on weaklings, and all three of them died young in terrible deaths, one in prison, one in a car crash, one cut his throat with a hunting knife. I feel guilty because it's exactly what I wished for them when I ran away from them. I got a lousy education here and I was an indifferent student, but I got very lucky in my 20s and after I wrote a bestselling book, everybody was proud of me. Not people here in town but all over the country. I got invited to speak at famous colleges and universities, I was admitted to elite organizations, I had dinner at the White House, and I started to think maybe my aunts were right—they thought I was smart—and then suddenly it was over, the line went dead. On account of a one silly video of me trying to deal with something in my nose—"

"The Harvard Phi Beta Kappa speech?"

I nodded.

"Oh, my god. I knew I'd seen you somewhere. I knew it. Oh, my god. That was the funniest thing I ever saw. Oh god. That look of concentration on your face. You were trying to look cool and casual but your finger was way up your nose. You looked like a little kid. And the pencil in the ear. And the strap up your crack. I'm sorry. I shouldn't laugh. Oh god." And she was laughing hard. She put her hand on my shoulder and put her head on it, she was laughing harder, big whoops and gulps and snorts, and then she quieted down, and then she let out another snort and her voice got higher, she was cackling and apologizing and gasping for breath, and I stood there quietly and gradually she stopped gasping and started apologizing.

"It's okay," I said. "Don't be sorry."

"I am. I'm a professional therapist, for god's sake. I'm not supposed to laugh at people's troubles, I'm supposed to help them heal."

But really, it was all right. She'd seen me in a ridiculous moment—three of them, actually—and I made her extremely happy, and that settles it. Even trade. Making people laugh is a high aspiration, one of the highest. It's what I most want to do with my life, though of course a man still needs to sleep and eat, though eating can be comical too, inexplicable spillage for example, split-pea soup on a striped-green shirt, think of it. My Harvard appearance gave her intense pleasure: why run away from success? Einstein squared mc and it equaled E, so that was it for relativity, nothing left for me to add, and I emceed a show and told stories about my relatives, and it amused people and never threatened to destroy the world. A man should be satisfied.

We stood on Main Street, looking at Bunsen Motors and the Unknown Norwegian across the street. I said, "I came back here to try to move on, and the past has me in its grip. I'm an old man, but some days I wake up and I'm 20 years old. I've been a writer since I was 20, and I still don't feel I've gotten it down on paper the way I should've."

"Gotten what down on paper?"

"Poetry."

"So you write poetry?"

I stood up straight and tall and said:

Life is one thing after another.
If you doubt me, just ask your mother.
Life proceeds from okay to terrible
Like a Shakespeare play or a Gospel parable.
Everyone marching to the same drummer
Into the night and the end of summer,
Toward old age and around the bend
To the page that says, "The End."
I could go on, but why should I bother?
Nothing to do except blame your father.
And yet I love to look around

At the lights of my hometown.
And take a breath of evening air,
Give thanks for the good we share
And bear the troubles we must bear.

"You wrote that?" she said.

"I did."

"Very nice."

We had come to Alice's house where Ashley was staying, and we stopped at the end of her sidewalk. An awkward moment, when you recite a poem of yours to a stranger and what can she say? Probably it happened to Shakespeare. He recited, "When in disgrace with fortune and men's eyes, I all alone beweep my outcast state," to the Dark Lady and she said, "Very nice. I like that." That's why Emily Dickinson didn't publish, she dreaded the thought of a neighbor saying, "I saw your poem about success being sweetest to those who ne'er succeed. Nice."

I was speechless. Ashley touched my arm. "You can't bring the past to life," she said. "You have to live your life in the present, same as everyone else."

That wasn't the point. The point is: I want to make something good out of my life. Something that will live on, like "Whose woods these are, I think I know" or "Since feeling is first, who pays any attention to the syntax of things will never wholly kiss you" or "Just off the highway to Rochester, Minnesota, twilight bounds softly forth on the grass. And the eyes of those two Indian ponies darken with kindness." I don't want to be very nice, I want to write something that'll survive me. She stood a moment in the light of the streetlamp, and thank God

I hadn't had any cheese or I might've thrown myself at her and thrown my arms around her, thinking I was in a novel and that's how the scene is supposed to go. Old men have feelings too and of course we work to stifle them because you can't walk up to strangers in the park and cry, "My heart leaps up when I behold a rainbow in the sky" just because the sunlight struck the moisture in the air a certain way. I refrained from embracing her. I missed my wife at that moment, the woman I can throw my arms around when so moved and she is bound by legal vows to accept this, it comes under the word "honor." I stood there like a fool, full of inexpressible feeling, as if I were 16 years old, and she said good night and went up the walk and into the house. We don't lock doors here. You'd think somebody'd walk in and shoot us, but I can't remember the last time somebody did. No, most of the worst things were self-inflicted.

13

A BEAUTIFUL CONVERSATION

Every marriage starts out as a scandal. Every romance is illicit in the eyes of the bride's brothers and the groom's sisters—he is beneath her—she entrapped him—she could do better than that—he never had much sense when it came to women. Daryl has known Marilyn since they were 14, and he took her walking in the summer and walked by a tree and in his great self-consciousness he whacked it with a stick and insects came down like rain and she threw herself screaming at him and he picked bugs off her and that's how it started, with extermination. He caught a dragonfly and showed her the beautiful scrollwork on its wings. Thus began a romance. He had no conversational skills because he'd always lived with people who knew more than he did, so what was there to say, but he gently picked bugs off her and it led to love, just as it does with other primates. Both families were dubious, but the ceremony put an end to it—*till death us do part*. Whammo. The chains are forged. People looked at each other during the reception and whispered, *Do you think it will last?* Maybe not. But they kept their doubts to themselves. And persistence and forgiveness won the day. And the acceptance of the inexplicable. He is a gardener and she is a reader. She lies in a hammock between a birch and a maple that he grew from saplings and she weeps for the Somali family in anguish waiting for the boat to take them to Greece as he trims the shrubbery and transplants the begonias and impatiens he bought at the greenhouse. She grieves for the cruelly oppressed in the midst of a paradise he has tended.

In the long-running marriage of Clarence and Arlene, her visits to old girlfriends in Minneapolis are sacred and her annual trip to New York with sisters Irene and Deanna to see shows and ride the ferry and eat at La Mirabelle, and likewise his weekly steak-and-eggs breakfast and his solo outings on his boat.

Clarence put his boat in the water on May 7th, the lettering on the stern faded but still readable: *O blessed boat, in which the weary weight of all the unintelligible world is lightened.* He put up a broad red umbrella and attached a reclining back to the rear seat where he could reach the electric outboard. He brought two cold Hummel beers and a salami sandwich and four of Arlene's ginger cookies and in his shirt pocket he had four cigarettes from his secret stash in the rafters of the garage. Arlene had taken the stepladder somewhere, so he had to stand on an unstable chair and reach way up high for the pack of smokes, and thought, *This would not be a good way to die, to fall and break my neck and be found with cigarettes around me, a man who gave his life for tobacco.* It felt good to push away from shore and then he saw a figure run out on the dock and wave to him and it was the therapist, Ashley. He grabbed hold of the dock and she climbed in. "Are you Clint?" she said. "I have you down for a two o'clock appointment."

He said, "No, I'm his older brother, Clarence, but anything you need to know from Clint you can probably get from me, we've been close all our lives even though we're sort of opposites. He's trying to be an atheist and I'm not."

She climbed into the bow seat and sat facing him, smiling, her face in shade under a straw hat, and he motored out along the sandbar and around Frenchman's Island and into the back bays where the bass fishermen like to lie in wait but nobody was there, just Clarence and a bright woman the age of his granddaughter. And what crossed his mind was, What if Hilmar's cheese affects me as it's affected others and I suddenly throw myself at her and babble endearments and I'm arraigned for attempted assault, will the cheese be an adequate defense, and even if it is, how will I live it down, a pariah, the object of righteous loathing, so I'd have to move to Minneapolis. The enormity of the danger staggered him. One minute you're at peace, the next in peril.

"What are you thinking?" said Ashley.

He said, "I'm thinking back to when I used to take a boat over here as a kid. Came over and smoked cigarettes. You mind if I have one?"

She laughed, and when he offered her one, she took it. He lit it. He gave her a beer and two ginger cookies.

She said, "I haven't had a smoke since I was at Augsburg College. I had a girlfriend and she and I had a band called Sapphic Traffic, kind of a goddess funk band. It was fun. I was majoring in religion but I was living a free life, studying scriptures all day and smoking dope at night and oh god the stuff we did. I was 19. She was 22. Cannabis, strunk, 422, Jefferies, Pacheco, lysergic acid, jiggybums, poojie, primo weed. She led me down the path and I was glad to follow. I'm amazed to still be alive. I broke up with her because I didn't love her, I just liked the stuff we did, and our band played in little clubs full of teen drunks and rich kids trying to find themselves. Being lesbian was a good way to keep from being hit on by guys, but then I took a psych course and suddenly everything became so real, the drugs faded away and I got an internship at a therapy clinic and I loved it. It's a way of being invisible, you know? You get to be a friendly stranger and people tell you their stories. I'm sorry. I came out here to talk to you and now I'm just jabbering. How long you been living here in Lake Wobegon?"

It was a sweet afternoon. Three hours, talking nonstop. He'd never done that before. He told her about his sophomore year at the University, loving his math and physics courses, and in April his mother called and said, "You've got to come home, your father has cancer and he doesn't have long." So he left school and his father took two years to die, while Clarence took over Bunsen Motors and ran it and his dream of teaching math went up in smoke and he became a Ford salesman instead. "I came back to run the business after my dad caught cancer. What was worse, he lost his English that winter, which he was proud of, having come from Stavanger when he was 17 and started up a business. But he went ice fishing that February in his fish house and a fisherman in a nearby fish house caught a four-pound walleye, pulled it up out of the hole, pulled the hook from its jaw, whereupon the fish flopped free and dove into the hole and the man's dog dove in the hole after him. He chased the fish under the ice, couldn't catch him, and finally, about to suffocate, he burst up through the hole in Dad's fish house, and the shock of a big black Labrador bursting up and knocking over a kerosene heater and Dad's fish house going up in flames—Dad couldn't speak English after that. And my Norwegian was child's talk. It took him forever to die, he was a tough old bird, and he didn't like the way I ran the business and he was angry about dying and he cursed me in Norwegian, and that was my enduring memory of Papa Bunsen. Norwegian has a big supply of profanity. I hated him when he died. I was glad to see him go. And I never took to cursing. 'Oh fiddle' is pretty strong for me."

He married Arlene because she was kind and eager to marry. Had his dad not gotten sick, Clarence would've married Peggy whom he'd been dating at the U, a journalist, but she had no interest in settling in a small town, she was headed for New York where journalism could be practiced at a fierce level, so it was Arlene instead. He walked up the aisle in a bright blue tux, thinking this was the biggest mistake of his life, and maybe it was, but he was brought up to make the best of things, so he did. He thought of Peggy sometimes, but she had married a German and vanished. Sometimes he felt he was in a play about a marriage, watching himself say the lines, but it was okay. They had worked out a happy arrangement whereas his son Duane married in haste and repented at leisure.

Ashley listened to that and told him about her mother's depression and how it lingered for years until finally she hanged herself in the garage one bright summer morning. Ashley was 14. They had a pleasant breakfast, Ashley went to swim class, came home to find the police and the coroner. She told him that her dad was a liar and adulterer but she loved him dearly. She said she liked Lake Wobegon a lot but wasn't sure if she was doing any good or not. She said, "I don't have solutions for people's problems, I only try to help them understand why things happen this way, and most of the time I'm just guessing."

 Clarence was dizzy with the pleasure of confession. He wished he had better stuff to confess, an affair of some sort, but no. He had inherited caution from his mother, and it bound him tightly still. Arlene was his one and only lover. But Peggy was a sometime fantasy, and, as a Christian, he considered fantasy to be sinful too, maybe even more hurtful.

She said, "I wish I believed in something, really believed in it. I think you're a believer."

"I suppose I must be."

"Do you believe that cheese is the cause of all this?"

"I do."

"Not repression?"

"No. We're comfortable with being private. My daughter Barbara Ann sat me down once and told me all about how troubled she was and distant she felt and unappreciated by coworkers and how unsatisfying her marriage was, and it sounded like bragging to me."

It was a fine afternoon and it gave him food for thought. Why did it come as such intense pleasure, to have a free-floating conversation? Why was this such a rare event in his life? It wasn't the confession of his disappointment by his father's death that deprived him of a math career. That was water under the bridge. Maybe it was age. At 75, you're quite aware of boundaries. You know that in this vale of tears, you have only so many confidantes and no more, and his closest confidantes had been Pastor Tommerdahl and Charlie Faust the history teacher, both long gone from this life, not to be replaced. And yet here was this woman of 28, hired to help the town work through its trauma, and she had given him three hours of lively honest interchange that felt miraculous. Her matter-of-factness about her mother and father, her sexuality, her drug habits, her career, he found admirable in the extreme, though it was something that people in this town avoid at all costs. But for all the pleasure it affords, what good does it do? *There's much to be said for stoicism*, he thought to himself. She hopped off at the dock and waved and trotted away, and he walked home.

"Where were you?" said Arlene.

"Went out in the boat."

"Oh. Run into anybody?"

"Nope. Just ate my lunch and came home."

"I'll never understand what is the pleasure of sitting in a boat."

She was fixing supper, salmon steaks and a salad. He stood behind her at the stove and put his hand on her shoulder.

"What?" she said.

"Smells good," he said.

"It's just salmon. You've had salmon before."

He got a bottle of Chardonnay out of the fridge and two wine glasses and unscrewed the cap.

"What's the occasion?"

"It's Monday." He poured two glasses half full.

He wanted to open his heart to her but of course he couldn't talk about Ashley and how delightful that had been, but what if someone had seen him with Ashley and Arlene finds out, he will now be assumed guilty of adultery, and maybe he is, and he wished that Charlie Faust were around to talk to, but he is gone. A brain tumor. In that brain was a thick file labeled Bunsen and it died with him and can't be duplicated. And then the doorbell rang.

He didn't want to answer it, but after the second ring she said, "Do you want me to answer the door?" so he went and there was a tall young man in a cheap suit who wanted to talk about the three angels in the book of Revelations and the Latter Days and soon the Tribulation, then the Second Coming and the beginning of the Millennium. The young man spoke very fast, thrusting his Bible at Clarence, pointing to verses, one after another. He knew his stuff, no hesitation. The more he talked, the happier he got. Revelations excited him. He trembled at the mention of the Tribulation. Clarence thought, Why is he so full of certainty and I'm so full of hesitation? He accepted a pamphlet, "The Seven Pillars of Truth," and thanked him, and when he finally got the door shut and the bolt locked, Arlene was at the table, eating her salmon, and there was no more conversation to speak of between them. The TV sat on the table and a man was talking about the economy booming and the two of them listened to him. The TV was there to prevent conversation. It wasn't a medium, it was a wall.

14

FAREWELL, O YOUTH

May 17th came along, Norwegian Independence Day, Syt-tende Mai, celebrating the day Norway threw off the yoke of Swedish oppression in 1814. At one time there had been a major parade in town by the Sons of Knute, the Grand Oya and his court with the Keeper of the Keys and the Lieutenants of Larvik dressed in all their silken finery and plumage, their gilded swords and horned helmets and capes and sashes and medals and ribbons, marching *whomp whomp whomp* in big black boots and singing "Helse dem dar hjemme," which teenage sat-irists sang as "What the hell, have an enema," but the parade had diminished with each generation and the diminishment was keenly felt by old-timers. Clarence had been a Knute and he'd tried to interest his son Duane but it was no go, what was a festive day to the father was a clown show to the son. So the costumes and swords and helmets were wrapped in tissue and stored in the basement of The Mercantile. Mr. Bakken, how-ever, gathered with other bachelors at the Chatterbox, passed the cheese around, sang "Kan Du Glemme Gamle Norge?" (Can

You Forget Old Norway?) and devoured their fried herring and potatoes, brooding about better days. "They're coming for me and my cheese," he said. "I can feel it. First they tell the jokes, then they destroy your traditions. I want to fight them to the death, but what'll happen to the dogs when I'm gone? They'll become fish food. Son of a bitch. A man can't live his own life in this world."

"Tellwith'm," said Berge. "Tellwithalov'm. Goddammumall t'hell. I got no idea why I'm still here. I never wanted to see the day when Syttende Mai means squat and nobody cares to sing the old songs. It's a damn shame is what it is. I was hoping to die in January. Cold as hell and Eddie called and said that the old regalia was for sale, take your choice, all the robes and sashes, and I said, That's it. Time to turn out the lights. Somebody could buy up the stuff and use it for trick-or-treating at Halloween. Our granddads and great-granddads wore the colors, and it would kill me to see teenagers traipsing around, wearing it as a big joke—Ha ha ha ha—so I went out and sat in the car. Not a bad way to die, freezing to death, probably the easiest for you and whoever has to clean up afterward. No mess, no odor, and the rigidity of the corpse makes for easier transportation. No rush to get you to an embalmer either, so your survivors have time to shop around for the best price. So I sat there waiting to die, and then I remember who it is who's going to bury me and inherit everything and it's my nephew Trey. Got no kids of my own and he's the one who stays in touch and remembers my birthday, so he's the heir. He lives over in Cottonwood. I forgot to give him a list of the people I don't want to come to the funeral. It's a long list, People I'd Rather Didn't Come, People Who Can

Come But Sit In Back, and People Who If I'd Known They Were There I'd've Dropped Dead. I left the list in the kitchen, under the silverware tray. I started to think about what my bank balance was, and I remember I hadn't looked at it in about four months and I thought I should take a look. I was close to death and I thought, "What the hell does it matter?" But it did matter. It was on my mind. So I staggered back to the house, no feeling in my hands or feet, and there was the bank statement, and I see I'm worth $41,425 and I think, "What in hell is Trey going to do with that kind of money? Probably marry the Tollefson girl and go live with her and her family. Her dad is on the list of People I'd Rather Not Come. Trey'd be living with them, and bet your bottom dollar he'd spend that money on new furniture and a rider lawn mower and his father-in-law'd be driving my good truck. And that did it. Ixnay on that. I tossed back a shot of Everclear, and Trey never came around to see me until a week ago and to hell with him."

Two weeks later, graduation came along and the Class of 2020 filed onto the football field as cell phones flashed and the band played "Pomp and Circumstance" and people dabbed at their eyes as the choir sang:

Hail to thee, our alma mater
Would that we might dwell
Longer in thy hallowed hallways,
But we bid farewell.

Long life's dangerous, lonely passages
Through the clouds of grief and fear

157

In our hearts we'll e'er remember
How you loved and taught us here.

Mr. Halvorson sat through the valedictorian's speech—about marching to a different drummer and daring to be yourself and do your part to light a candle and brighten the darkness that comes before the dawn and make a difference in the world because it's the only one we have—and as he sat there, he noticed the woman in the second row, fourth from the left. Every year at graduation, the senior boys fulfill their obligation to play a joke on the administration. They've done bottle rockets, they've made the sound system get warbly and trebly, and one year, a flatulent stench drifted over the crowd, thanks to a kid with a gift for chemistry. One year, hundreds of frogs came hopping across the grass. Last year, they loosened the brakes on the lectern so that it rolled off the stage, and when he reached into his pocket for his speech he found an envelope full of mashed potato. And now he looked into the crowd of graduates and recognized the woman in the fourth row as a waitress from Charlie's in Freeport, looking very determined, fiddling with the zipper on her gown, and he had a strong hunch he was going to be flashed by her, he could see senior boys smirking at each other—he hoped the poor woman had been paid well and in advance.

He stood up to address the graduates as he does every year, but this year he felt odd, his smile was gone and his voice felt tight. He congratulated them on their hard work and good citizenship and then he said, "You're leaving a comfortable world for a world of grief and disappointment for which you are utterly unprepared. You've been educated to live in your parents' world, which doesn't exist anymore. Most of what you've learned is already outdated and the rest is irrelevant. Your parents own more of the world than they should, and you will have to grab it out of their cold, grasping fingers. If you're lucky, they'll get premature dementia and it can't be premature enough. Book learning is mostly useless. Most of what we know we learn by keeping our eyes open. You've been brought up to follow the rules and respect your elders, but the rules are changing and your elders are standing in your way. Nonetheless, they're the gatekeepers in this world, they run powerful corporations and rule over universities, and so you need to weasel your way around them unless you intend to be outlaws and terrorists. My advice is: avoid the liberal arts, it is a road to mediocrity. The best education available is the Army or Navy or Marines. After that comes science and engineering. Some of you imagine you'll be songwriters or poets or actors. The only reason to go into the arts is to impress girls. The U.S. Post Office is full of people who intended to be songwriters. Instead, they're running sorting machines. Just keep this in mind: high school is a prison camp designed to suppress your hormones and make you into passive followers. If you want to be free, you'll have to educate yourselves and don't wait too long. And remember, my generation is not your friend. When I was your age, we said, 'Never trust anybody over 30.' It's even more true today. Good luck. You're going to need it."

It was a stunning speech and people applauded politely, which goes to show how little attention is paid to graduation speeches—people hear platitudes even when there aren't any. The graduates marched up to the stage to get their diplomas and shook his hand and thanked him. And the waitress came across the stage, her zipper in hand, bracing herself, and he took her hand and said. "My darling, if you drop your gown, people will take pictures and they'll be everywhere and you may have to leave town. I'd think it over if I were you. How much did they pay you?" She said, "Two hundred bucks." He said, "Keep the money, no matter what. Laugh in their faces. If you want to go into pornography, do it in Los Angeles, the money is better. Okay? Good luck."

At the end of the ceremony, the class of 2020 stood and Mr. Halvorson stood and faced them. A notice had been sent to all of them, an order by the Board: *There will be no tossing of mortarboards at the conclusion of the ceremony and all who violate this order will be required to attend a one-week course in good citizenship in July before receiving a diploma.* He said, "I present to you the Class of Two Thousand and Twenty." A pause, and then every mortarboard was flung high in the air, to his great relief. A test of character had been passed.

The post-graduation parties were as festive as ever. Parents congratulated him as did members of the school board. They were distracted by late news that two members of the class of 2020 were engaged to be wed—the groom, a Krebsbach, would be pumping gas at Krebsbach Chev, and the bride, a Bunsen, would be attending the U to major in psychology, the first union between those two families, like a collie falling in love with a bulldog. Meanwhile, Mr. and Mrs. Halvorson drove home and when they got there, she said, "I can't believe what you said tonight," and when he said, "What?" and she told him, he was astonished. "Never trust anybody over 30? I said that?" She said,

"You have to write an apology." He said, "I'll think about it." But why apologize for something that apparently nobody paid attention to? It'll only draw attention to it. Anyway, summer was here and he could keep his distance until the effect of the cheese had worn off. "No more cheese," she said. "Not even Parmesan or cheddar."

15

WILDFLOWERS

The next day, a serenely beautiful summer day, the smell of new-mown hay in the air, and coconut suntan cream and bug spray, people on the beach, many of them not from here, you can tell because they show no tan line. They wear skinny swimsuits made of less cotton than in an aspirin bottle. People from around here are polar people, we don't tan, we burn. Duane Bunsen came home once with a model named Cherise who had a deep tan though it was only April. She was remarkable. Skinny, with a pouty mouth and breasts the size of gingersnaps. Her favorite word was "cool." She said it hundreds of times. She wore earbuds all day and carried a phone around, usually with somebody on the other end, not talking, just *being*. She brought a sun lamp and lay under it from time to time to keep her color. She had no need of language at all, only light. She was a plant, an exotic fern.

Nobody back in my day ever lay in the sun to get tanned, except some girls. Men worked in the sun and lay in the shade. And we didn't bother with air conditioners because if you worked in the sun long enough, the shade felt so good you didn't need frigidity. You work in the sun, even a little breeze is a pleasure. I have nothing against tanning and air-conditioning, I am only pointing out facts. As my mother liked to say, "Life has its ups and downs, so just make the best of it." We were designed to live in this world as it is, not the world as we wish it were. Air-conditioning is for invalids, a form of life support. As for winter, you simply need to know how to dress. Don't get me started.

When Roger Hedlund along with Clint Bunsen set out to battle the Keep America Truckin' Museum and Motorway, he hired a St. Paul lawyer to scout out some roadblocks to throw in its way, whereupon Dick Dixon sent a truckload of Harvard Law grads to grind them to pieces and spit them out. The local lawyer was a Concordia Law grad who believed in polite negotiation between gentlemen, not pouring boiling oil on your opponents and strewing their bodies on open fields for buzzards to snack on their testicles. Cooperation was Bob's goal, not evisceration. He had represented one husband in a divorce case, and the wife wound up with the mansion and both cars and Bob's client wound up with a pup tent and a three-speed bicycle. When it came to battle, he had no sword, only a wooden spatula.

Bob wrote the Dixon legal team a polite request for more information, and they responded with so many lawsuits against Clint and Roger, they had to buy a new file cabinet to store them in—tortious negligence, bilateral bifurcation, systematic pesterance, deleterious declarations, defamatory fraud, false pretenses, privation of assets, felonious failure of consideration, tainted tangibility, malicious mercantile cruelty, casual capriciousness, bequeathing in bad faith, breach of equity, evidentiary preponderance, and a $100 million lawsuit for impeding development. But as it turned out, their vast learning and acumen did not carry the day. As it turned out, Hilmar's band of wild dogs had the last word, and the lawyerly briefs stayed in the file cabinet.

Clint asked Pastor Liz to intervene with Hilmar, and she said, "You're the big atheist, I think you should talk to him," but Clint said no, Hilmar had a soft spot for her, so she drove out past the You Are Not Welcome sign. Hilmar was in his machine shed with a couple of young barn cats that he was castrating, and he said, "Here. Hold him." And Liz did, and Hilmar passed a little chloroform under the cat's nose and put him out and reached back between the hind legs and sterilized the razor in a candle and snipped the sac and dabbed it with alcohol and Liz felt suddenly light-headed but remained standing.

"You get too many cats and they get competitive and forget what they're here for, which is to be good mousers. Females are better at that, and males are pretty worthless. All they do is sniff around the females. Same as with people. Anyways, I'm preparing to move on. Don't tell anybody, but I got my eye on a place out west. I never been beyond Fargo, and I think it's time I saw some of the world while I can still navigate. You know why? Because I don't want to die here. I truly don't. I don't want to die, I want to disappear. I see myself going to a city I've never been in before, where I don't know a soul, and throwing away my billfold and my car keys and getting a room in a hotel and dying there in my sleep, and let that be the end of it. My mother said, 'Hilmar, don't you dare put me in the cemetery.'

She wanted to rise up in a cloud of smoke, so that's what I did for her. I wrapped her in a quilt and I put her in her old chicken house and collapsed it around her and cut the heads off of the last four chickens and laid them with her, and I dumped a truck-load of charcoal on it and about 40 gallons of kerosene, and at the stroke of midnight I tossed a torch on her and up she went and it burned for two days, and what was left I plowed into the ground and next year planted tomatoes and squash. She was 85. I'm 76. Time to think about making an exit. Don't wait too long, that's my advice." He reached for the next cat, applied the chloroform, held the razor to the flame, snipped the sac, and dabbed the antiseptic. "I had a pretty good life. People left me alone, I appreciate that. Now they're crowding in on me, and I understand, they can't help it. So it's time to go."

Liz came home from Hilmar's farm and parked in the church lot and saw Lenny walking toward her in a bright green pantsuit that Liz had donated to the school rummage sale. They stopped and talked. Lenny said she was leaving soon for Colorado—she'd identified the virus, the rest was up to Alice. Greg had been dumped by his folksinger, Sandy, who'd found herself a singing partner named Gene, and the next day Greg called Lenny and said he missed her and she told him he should get a dog with her color hair. He cried on the phone, which she'd never heard him do, on a phone or in person, but he didn't have the knack of crying, his was whiny and whimpering. She wished him well but was afraid he might come to Minnesota so she had to hustle.

The pantsuit looked joyful on her. Whenever Liz wore it, she felt like a walking pea pod. To see another woman look good in clothes that made her feel weird seemed like a possible sermon topic. But the next week she drove into St. Cloud with another load of used clothing. She was in a mood to lighten her possessions and move on.

She drove into the parking lot of the Crossroads shopping center and hauled the load over to a Goodwill donation dumpster and heaved her stuff in and heard the clink of car keys inside and climbed up to look into the dumpster and fell in and landed on her load. It was a deep dumpster and the lid closed on her and latched so she couldn't open it. She knocked on the lid but nobody came. And then a little girl named Kelly did. She asked Kelly to find a grownup to open the dumpster, and Kelly was afraid and Liz had to persuade her that she, Liz, was not a bad person. She told Kelly that she was a church minister and Kelly was not reassured. Liz sang, "This Little Light of Mine." She recited "Baa-baa Black Sheep." The child said, "Goodbye." Liz said, "Please. I won't hurt you. I promise. Please tell a grownup." And she sang "Ave Maria" in a loud clear voice, and a man opened the lid.

"I fell in," she explained. He helped her out and asked if she was okay. There was an intimation in his voice that she might've been drinking or on drugs or having an episode. It did not help matters when she explained about the car keys and he got a stick and poked around in the dumpster and didn't see them and then she said, "Oh, they're in my pocket."

She went back to her car and thought, "This'd be a wonderful story that you'd tell at your 10th wedding anniversary dinner, the story of how you met. You fell into a dumpster and he helped you out and you fell in love. But without the love affair, it's just a story about stupidity. Meaningless." Like the toilet seat story, she shuddered to recall. Had her parishioners truly forgiven her for that? She feared not. Dignity is high on the Lutherans' list of virtues. She drove home, and when she saw the "Woebegone" water tower, it dawned on her that an unmarried woman minister in a town this small was thereby committing herself to a bachelor life. A Lutheran bachelor minister. There were no available men her age in town. If she signs up for another two years, it'll turn into 10. She'll be 45. A middle-aged Lutheran minister is not a hot romantic prospect. She'd do better as a waitress.

In June, Dick Dixon himself flew to Lake Wobegon, traveling by helicopter from the Minneapolis airport. The chopper landed on the Pfleiderscheidt pasture, where a six-man video crew would shoot Mr. Dixon announcing the park and motorway, but what the pilot thought was the Pfleiderscheidts' was actually Hilmar Bakken's pasture and a pack of wild dogs came tearing out, slavering for human flesh, and unfortunately Mr. Dixon had halfway lowered himself out the cabin door. He was slower climbing up than coming down, being a weighty man, and two dogs got his pants in their jaws and tore the seat off and some meat along with it before the chopper could rise. Hilmar came tearing out the barn, and fired two shots that nicked the rotor shaft, snapping a steering cable, so that the chopper spun rather rapidly counterclockwise in the air, and by the time the pilot wrestled it under control, Mr. Dixon was not the commanding presence he had been 10 minutes before. The chopper managed to land in town at the ballpark, the only open space visible, about 50 feet behind second base, in the top half of the fourth inning, still slowly spinning, and Mr. Dixon emerged bottomless and confused and bleeding badly, and a thousand Whippet fans whooped and yelled, thinking it was a joke. He staggered, half crawled, to the infield and began to say how proud he was to be here in honor of a great man, and the Whippets trainer Jimmy Milton came out and tended to his wounds and made a catcher's chest protector into a butt protector, there being no pants Mr. Dixon's size (48), and a catcher's mask for his manhood. He limped out of the park to a standing ovation and found himself in downtown Lake Wobegon, dazed and disoriented, and walked down the middle of Main Street, attracting a good deal of attention, especially when the butt protector fell off. That was the picture that appeared on the wire services, under the headline "Public Rebuttal." Wally took him into the Sidetrack Tap and poured him a Wendy's stout, and the tycoon launched into what sounded like a campaign speech in which he pledged to make America great before his staff found him and led him away.

Mr. Dixon stayed around for a couple days and went to work on Hilmar, who refused to talk to him but talked to a Dixon lawyer who visited him with a grocery bag full of bundles of hundreds. Hilmar said no, but he weakened as the offer climbed past two million to three and then five, a high price for 60 acres of piss-poor pasture. "What about the house?" he said. "What happens to that?" They promised to make it a sacred site in the park, surrounded by a secure fence. "People'd try to get into it," he grumbled. They promised him No Admission, or Paid Admission, or Select Admission, whatever he wished. He asked for a week to think it over.

The Hoerschgens sold their farm for two and a half million,

and they came and thanked Hilmar for driving the price so high. Ardis threw her arms around him and said she and Arlen were on their way to their son Dennis's place in Camino de la Costa, California, where he'd found a fine house for them overlooking the sea and a beach with sea lions, and she played Hilmar a video on her phone of the waves rolling in, the flagstone terrace and pool, the pink stucco house, the cliff beyond. "We owe it all to you," she said. Hilmar said, "You don't owe me nothing. What're they doing with your house?" Ardis said, "We're taking some clothes and some pictures and the good china and that's it. Leaving in an hour. Done with it. Arlen needs a heart valve repair. Dennis has a surgeon lined up in San Diego."

They honked and she waved as they drove away, and within minutes a demolition crew came and tore down the Hoerschgen house and barn and outbuildings. Hilmar was milking that afternoon when a Holstein switched him in the face with its tail, which had fresh fecal matter on it, and he slugged her in the forehead and knocked her out and she fell over on him and it took him a while to squirm out from under. He heard derisive mooing as he slid out. He finished milking, but he sensed that the herd had turned against him. He walked down the narrow path between the rows of rumps, and tails lifted and cows excreted with surprising accuracy and some tried to kick him. He could hear them that night, discussing things among themselves, conspiring against him, and in the morning it felt for certain like they were laying for him, waiting to catch him and butt him up against a wall and lean him to death. It took all the pleasure right out of dairy farming. The two reindeer, Dasher and Dancer, were following him too closely, poking him with their horns, treading on his heels, and he detected an attitude of resentment. He had never felt threatened by livestock before, but something was up in the farmyard, he could hear it in their bellowing. They knew he was selling the place and not taking them along, and they meant to stop him. That evening, the reindeer jumped the fence and left for parts unknown. He didn't wait around for further developments. He called the packing plant, and they sent over two trucks to haul the herd off to slaughter. He stood by the ramp as the cows were loaded up and he explained it to them. "You crossed a line when you crapped on me. I don't take shit from cows. So you're going to be stunned with a high-voltage shock, your throats cut, you'll be skinned and butchered. Have a nice trip." The trucks disappeared over the hill and he felt exhilarated. Free, for the first time in his life. His dogs sat in the dirt, confused at the disappearance of the cows, and he took mercy on them. He fed them 16-ounce filet mignons with crushed sleeping pills inside. They feasted and fell asleep, and he cut their throats and laid their bodies in his mother's little house and stacked logs and old lumber around them and threw in a torch and it went up in a funeral pyre worthy of Viking warriors, a blaze that could be seen in town. The firetruck came racing out but he waved them away. The dogs died happy, and nobody would ever touch his mother's things. He called the Dixon lawyer, and he brought the money, a bag of rolls of hundreds and a certified check. Hilmar signed the bill of sale, the deed, and climbed into his pickup. "Anything from the trailer?" the lawyer said. Hilmar shook his head, got in the truck, drove out past the YOUR LIFE IS NOT MY FAULT sign and didn't look back.

16

MR. DIXON EATS THE CHEESE

The demolition crew dug a pit and pushed the mobile home into it and the wreckage of the house and torched the barn and sheds, and then turned their attention to the Hoer-schgen meadow, which would become part of the parking lot. A small city of trailers set up overnight in the Bakken pasture. An architect and a battalion of engineers arrived. Designers in linen suits held up the blueprints, surveyors surveyed, stakes were pounded in. A bulldozer went to work on the Hoerschgen meadow, the field of wildflowers, the prayer station established by the Purses, and as the dozer blade hit the stone wall, flames burst up and a gaping hole opened in the earth and the dozer plunged in as the driver leaped out with a shout. The excavating crew probed the hole and found nothing; the earth had swallowed the bulldozer whole. A crowd of suits discussed options and decided to try dynamite. A crate of explosives was lowered into the hole and there was a low rumbling sound and suddenly sticks of dynamite came flying out and the suits scattered in all directions. They tried flamethrowers, they dumped truckloads of boulders, they dumped boiling water, they poked a seismic device on a long arm into the hole and heard ominous rumbling and gurgling that got louder and then they ran for their lives as red-hot lava came bubbling and burgeoning up. The smell was indescribable. Acrid, fetid, pungent, sulfurous, noxious, rank, dank, and what's more, it spread steadily to cover 50 acres.

Mr. Dixon's team contacted the U.S. Geological Survey in the Department of the Interior in Washington, and a team of scientists was convened, meetings held, a preliminary study issued, a long list of likelihoods outlined, a work timetable extending into 2022. This was unacceptable and a Dixon man got connected by way of his brother-in-law to an assistant secretary who, like the brother-in-law, was an elder in the Assembly of Apostolic Unity, as was the secretary himself, the A.A.U. having been crucial early supporters of the Trump movement. Believers in the imminence of the Second Coming—"imminence" meaning less than a year—the A.A.U. had brought a stop to climate change research and other long-term studies for the simple reason that Jesus would soon be taking his true believers to heaven and unbelievers would simply have to fend for themselves. The secretary believed that the world is in its Final Dispensation, the Rapture but a month or two away, and so no further scientific research is necessary, only the acceptance of revelation, although he was willing to consider exceptions to the policy if there were tangible evidence of grace. The Dixon man said that geological research was of utmost importance so the motorway and memorial park could be built, and he asked what might constitute tangible evidence of grace and the assistant secretary rubbed his thumb and forefinger together, and two weeks later, Mr. Dixon held a $100,000-per-head Republican fundraiser at the Trump Mirage International Hotel at which very important people were present who could certainly help him solve his lava problem.

He rented the ballroom of the Trump Mirage and engaged a band to play Johnny Rogers's patriotic numbers, and there was an elaborate buffet, including giant shrimp and squid in an unusual cheese sauce that the French chef thought was a great delicacy, Portuguese cheese, and so as not to seem provincial, people praised it lavishly, though it left them feeling slightly confused.

Then a bell dinged and Mr. Dixon came to the microphone and, as reported by the Fake News and the failing New York *Times,* he thanked everyone for coming and said, "You, like me, are 150 percent behind our president, and ever shall be as we were in the beginning. Draining the swamp, maintaining our borders, ending Obamacare, cutting taxes, bringing the genius of free enterprise to government, cutting federal aid to the urban shitholes, pulling out of international alliances that have been robbing us blind for years—I am totally in favor. If there are any liberals here, be careful who you stand in front of—there are armed men here and very bad things might happen." He chuckled and felt faint nausea and took a glass of water and his voice got a little higher. "I say this as a patriotic American, not as a personal friend of our president. In fact, I'm not sure he has any. Let's be honest here. The man has never told a joke, he can't bear to be touched, and when was the last time you saw him smile like he meant it? Dogs and cats are averse to him, small children shrink back. The man grew up in a shell. For a business guy, he's not good with numbers so he made up his own balance sheets. He was born rich so he attracted beautiful girls who played him like a fish on a line. The man couldn't push a wheelbarrow in a straight line, but he had dough coming out of his pockets—if he dropped a Ben Franklin, he wouldn't bother to pick it up, so he attracted hangers-on, skinheads and beach bums and biker boys. His fear of physical contact isn't about germs, it's because he got poked in the snoot once and had no idea what to do about it. The thought of rassling makes him dizzy, so now he's got other men to do it for him. He tweets, that's as rough as he gets. We never had a tweeter for president before. Anyway, that's neither here nor there. As I say, I am a major supporter all the way.

"What I don't understand is the look, the style. That mod look, the cut of the suit, the long tie, is out of the '70s. Vintage, but the wrong vineyard. Who is his tailor? Sears Roebuck? And the makeup. My God. A president who wears lip gloss and foundation and eyeliner? This man is commanding our troops? And the Nancy-pansy hairdo with the hairspray to keep the little swoops and swirls in place. Gay liberation is a done deal: you don't have to declare yourself with your hair, you can just say, 'I'm gay. Vote for me, sweetheart.'

"Anyway, I'm proud to be on his side. Ignore the makeup, the man is a genius as he himself has said." And then Mr. Dixon stopped and whispered to his wife, "Where am I? Who are these people?"

Long story, short: there were a dozen men in the crowd who picked up their phones and called the White House and the next day Dixon Trucking came under very close inspection by the Federal Motor Carrier Safety Administration, which found a couple loose lug nuts on a truck in Nashville and pulled all of Dixon's thousand trucks off the roads for inspection, which turned up some loose seat cushions and flaking paint and muffler violations and untinted windshields and fines were levied, and there was no telling when the inspections would end, and Mr. Dixon, already millions in debt for the Johnny Rogers project, on the advice of his accountants, put the whole thing up for auction, and a Saudi company found itself owning a couple thousand acres of Minnesota and donated it to the Izaak Walton League for conservation, which was pleased to find 50 acres of wildflowers blooming in the meadow where the dozer had disappeared, including a number of never-before-identified species, one of which, a variety of lily, was named Arvonne. So many colors: you squinted and you could imagine a crowd of a thousand men in crazy sportcoats, the annual meeting of Mormon maritime insurance salesmen, the clothing racks of Montgomery Wards, the money managers of Helena, Montana, or the Maine Men's Minuet Movement. That summer, Father Powers established a nine-hole pitch-and-putt on the Bakken farm, and sometimes a golfer hooked a shot into the wildflowers and no balls thus hit were ever recovered—it became the Amen Corner.

17

BE GLAD

Marlon was disappointed that the petition for beatification of Sister Arvonne had gone nowhere, the archbishop in St. Paul was indifferent to it, nobody ever presented it to the cardinal in St. Louis. Father Powers had promised to take it up with His Eminence. "He was waiting for the right moment," Marlon said. "He's golfing with a papal nuncio next month. If he senses an opening, he'll jump on it." But the requisite posthumous miracles simply weren't there. Myrtle told me that Florian had finally agreed to sell off his implement collection and sell the farm and move to a high-rise, and she said she had prayed to Arvonne about it, but real estate transactions hardly count as miracles. And the genuine and authentic miracle of Arvonne's wildflowers—the devouring of a bulldozer and spitting forth of hot lava in defiance of geological science—the evidence had effaced itself.

Clint Bunsen was secretary of the Izaak Walton board and he liked to walk with Fred out into the mass of colors, the air engorged with sweetness. Hardy plants in such profusion you could walk on them without injuring them, something he'd never done before. He sat in the field and breathed deeply, he lay back, flowers around his head, and the bee did not sting nor did the mosquito bite. Fred was at peace, as well. And Clint heard a quiet voice say, "Seek and you shall find, ask and it shall be given unto you." He didn't hear it so much as he felt it. A still small voice. Maybe nobody else would've heard it but he did. He told Irene and she told him to write down what he heard, so he did.

Let someone else do the work. Sit down and listen.
Come into the field with thanksgiving and into the flowers
with praise.
You dropped your wallet.
I am not wrathful.

He sat on the spot where the bulldozer had been swallowed up into the earth and dynamite spit out and boulders erupted and red-hot lava and now it was a field of flowers, a resplendent miracle, especially to one who'd spent so many hours on a roller platform looking up at the underside of Ford cars and trucks.

Clint walked around the field, stopped where the stone wall had stood, where so many of the faithful had knelt and prayed for impossibilities. Fred sniffed the ground. Clint wondered if his mind was playing with him, teasing him. The brain has great powers of imagination. He'd grown up listening to scripture, and now an inventive circuit of his brain with a gift for imitation was streaming a few Great Inspirational Quotes his way. Did all atheists have these jokes played on them? He walked down the hill to the Bakken property and stood where the Bakken doorstep had been. He said, "Irmgaard, you were a woman of faith and you endured Olaf's bad habits and you raised Hilmar, who loved you to death and took the path of unbelief, you of whom my Grandma Bunsen said, She finds joy where others see despair—show me the way out of my confusion, I pray you, in the name of our Savior, assist me."

Good of you to mention me. Irmgaard is occupied at the moment, you can talk to me directly.

"It would help if I had someone to talk to. If this is a vision, why can't I see someone?"

Don't look up. Look down.

He looked down and there was Fred looking up. "I can speak through birds, bears, a lion—how's this?" the dog said.

"Nobody will believe me if I tell them."

"Don't tell them. I'm talking to you, I can talk to them some other time."

He wished there were clouds, mist, maybe a rainbow. Why not a great radiant figure, bearded, in biblical robes, sitting on a mountain? Okay, it's Minnesota, but He's God, why not a mountain? He did not see how he could tell Irene, "I went out to the Bakken farm and Fred spoke to me with the voice of God."

"I know what you're thinking," the dog said, "and it's strange for me too." There was a look in the dog's eyes as if he had eaten something odd and was trying to decide if he liked it or not.

"Please don't bring harm to my family," said Clint. "I believe you are God, you don't have to be dramatic. I believed before and now I believe again. Glory be to the Father and to the Son and to the Holy Ghost. As it was in the beginning, is now and ever shall be. Amen."

"Amen," said the dog. "Did you hear about the man who comes to God and he says, 'Lord, is it true that to you a million dollars is as one penny, and a thousand years is as one second?' And God said, 'Yes, my son.' And the man said, 'Could I have a million dollars?' And God said, 'Sure. Just a second.'"

Clint didn't laugh.

"The man who wrote that joke died a few days ago, and I told him I was an admirer. Josephson was his name. Jewish, like me. He was a comedian who never had the success he deserved, and he worked for peanuts in a lot of scuzzy clubs and his routines were all about marital problems and lousy jobs so there was no place for a God joke and he never used it. He tried for years to get on TV and wound up in telemarketing, selling crummy retirement schemes, poor guy. He was impressed that I knew his joke. I said, 'How come you didn't ask me for more material?' I said, 'I write a lot of comedy myself.' 'Really?' he says. 'Yeah. Really. *The rivers run into the sea and yet the sea is not full.* That's mine. *Whoever increases knowledge increases sorrow.* Solomon got the credit but I wrote it. *The thing that has been is the thing that shall be; and the thing that is done is that which shall be done: there is nothing new under the sun.* That's comedy in a nutshell. Isn't that the way you say it? 'In a nutshell?'"

"Yes, sir."

"One perfect joke is worth more to me than a thousand insincere prayers and you can quote me on that. Did you hear about the man who is dying of liver cancer and he smells his wife taking a lemon meringue pie out of the oven, his favorite pie, and he crawls out of bed and into the kitchen and there it is on the counter. He grabs a knife and fork, and his wife hits him hard upside the head and she says, 'That's for the funeral. Leave it alone.' He says, 'But lemon meringue is only good for a day or two.' She says, 'As I said, it's for the funeral.' That is a good joke."

"I need to get home," Clint said. "Thanks for the information. Come, Fred."

The dog looked up at him intently. "There are other things I'd like to talk about but the musculature of a dog's lips and tongue are such that it's hard to make myself understood," he said.

"The what?"

"Musculature."

"What?"

"Musculature."

"Musculature?"

"Yes. There are other things I could speak of but cannot due to an imperfect vessel."

"What else would you like to talk about?" said Clint.

The dog looked down at the ground and with his right paw he carefully made the letters. *E-s-c-h-a-t-o-l-o-g-y.* "Be happy," the dog said. "Bless your house and your people. Know that you're loved. Do good for evil. You know the rest. Goodbye."

He went home, the dog by his side, and that evening, when Irene put dinner on the table, he took her hand in his and said a prayer over the food. "That was lovely," she said. "I'm glad you're back to doing that."

"After what I've seen, it's the least I can do," he said.

The next morning, he returned to the meadow with a bag of tape cassettes. Fred was too exhausted to come along, he could not be roused from his bed. Clint had taped dozens of podcasts by the atheist lady, Michelle, who reminded him of his sister Lizzie, abrupt and to the point. He listened to her in the car on his way out to Hoerschgens' farm. She said, "The only one who can tell you who you are is the small voice within, not the big voice in the sky. The solution to our problems is to fulfill our own humanity, not seek the favor of an ancient god who promised to murder the Israelites' competitors if the Jews would flatter him and avoid shellfish. Our childlike dependency on this deity, sometimes generous, sometimes vengeful, is a huge roadblock in our own maturation. It's time to accept reality and accept that *this is it—what you see*—you don't leave here and climb into Daddy's lap. The golden gate is in San Francisco and when you go through it, you're out to sea." It was very well said and had no relevance anymore. He took the bag of cassettes out to the field and heaved it high in the air into the wildflowers and walked over to where it had landed and there was no sign of it.

18

FINDING THE SPANGLER HOUSE

Lenny called me the day the Walton conservancy announced the cancellation of the motorway and park to say congratulations. "I had nothing to do with it," I said. "It was Hilmar's dogs and the cheese that Dixon ate and the miracle of the flowers that ate the Caterpillar. That miracle should've won sainthood for Sister Arvonne, but the problem is—nobody prayed to her to ask for it, she just did it on her own."

Lenny said she was about to leave town, and if I wanted her to come along and visit the old Spangler house and see if my 1967 red Mustang was still there, tonight might be her only available time. She said, "I'm quitting epidemiology. My public health service down in Dallas reorganized itself and epidemiology has been merged with dermatology and periodontism in one department called Task Force Two, so I asked for severance and got a hundred grand and the house sold for 250, so I'm moving to Aspen and taking up painting."

"How's Greg?" She said Greg had taken up chemical dependency full-time and was living in a basement with a laptop, a fridge, and a microwave, and writing angry incoherent posts about political correctness on Facebook. "I used to resent men and their special privileges, and now that I've seen a number of them fall apart, I feel sorry for them. You belong to a fragile gender and it happens around the age of 60, the contradictions tear them apart. I wish I could help but I'm busy. But when do I get to read your book?"

"Never," I said. "I stopped working on it. It got too weird and tangled up. I don't understand it anymore."

"Sorry to hear it. Anyway, pick me up at seven at my mom's and I'll come with you and look for that car."

It was a red fastback Mustang, 5-speed manual transmission, power steering. I borrowed it from a guy named O'Neill who needed to go back to Tipperary to see his granny who was dying but who recovered when she laid eyes on him, so he stayed and let me keep the car. After Lake Wobegon I planned to drive to California and settle down in Napa and sit on a mountain and give up material things including the Mustang if he ever came back again.

Lenny and I headed up the deserted road toward the brick mansion where I had jumped out the window to escape the woman hitchhiker back in 1969. Lenny said she wanted to believe my story, but whether she did or not, she was curious about that house. She had heard stories about it too, stories about bad children who'd been locked up for misbehavior and lived in tiny filthy cells with cockroaches and rabid mice, weeping behind their barred windows, living on crusts of dried bread until they were released to live in foster homes in cities out west where they joined work gangs in the lettuce fields. She had been a light-hearted child, but hearing those stories turned her toward doing good in the world. She wanted to cure disease and teach good hygiene to others. "A true epidemiologist never shakes hands or eats in a restaurant or uses public transportation," she said. We don't go to concerts, we listen to music at home and we sterilize the headphones.

We found the brick house, which now appeared to be occupied and rather fancy. The yard was well-groomed, there was a statue of a bearded man with a fence around it. And in fact, it was much larger than it had been in 1969. There was a long wing extending from the side and another wing branching off from that wing, each of them much larger than the original, and I thought I could see other similar structures back in the trees. And then I noticed the sign: Broadmoor. And an electronic voice said: *Approach the gate slowly.* It came from a small box on a steel post. So we walked to the front door and it opened slowly.

"I can't go in, I'm sorry," said Lenny. "I am terrified. Everyone has her limits. This is mine. My heart rate—" she looked at a monitor on her wrist—"is 105. I'll wait here. I promise I won't leave. If anything happens to you, I'll run for help.

"Be careful," she said.

I went through the door, it was almost dreamlike, and the house was very orderly, institutional, and so was the woman who beckoned me into her office. She looked like someone I might've had for a teacher in eighth-grade geography, no nonsense, in a uniform with no insignia, every hair in place, clean as a whistle. She said, "I take it you have some familiarity with our goals and strategies here, so if you'd be so good as to sign this, we can get started." She passed me a paper and without looking at it, I signed the bottom line. She gave me a glass of water.

She said, "So you're familiar with our philosophy of breaking through cultural and attitudinal clutter and going straight to the paradigm of self-esteem, which you desperately want and of course we want for you. Our team of partners has looked over your history and they have formulated a quadrangular road map of (1) proactive empowerment, (2) centricity rather than linearity, (3) leveraged wellness, and (4) sustainable synergy. In other words, enablement. Any questions?" Her phone buzzed then and she said, "Yes?" and a man at the other end asked her something about bandwidth and she turned her back and looked at a green computer screen, and I quietly stood up and walked out of the building. I didn't run; I walked briskly. A moderate trot. "Who's in there?" said Lenny. "It's some sort of hospital, I think, but it may be a religion, I can't be sure. Anyway, it's not for me." We walked for half a mile down the road, and I recognized it as the road I'd driven down back in 1969. And there, beyond a grove of big birch trees, was the red Mustang parked exactly where I'd left it 50 years ago. My textbooks were still in the front seat and notebooks with my notes on Chaucer and American Literary Journalism and the U.S. Constitution and my journal written with a fountain pen, black. I read it to her aloud:

I must learn to take people as they are, and life as it is. My fate is to be friendless and to accept the emptiness of existence. I have longed to be united with an Other and there is no one for me: a fact and it must be lived with. Why do I imagine otherwise? All I have is words. My life is a tragic joke. I imagine I am a writer but all I have are these incoherent superficialities. There is no way out except to cease to exist and this will happen soon enough. Each passing

*day is calling me to a cruel fate. The world closes in as it
has closed in on others. A great silence surrounds me and
I will walk down the road and be forgotten, as millions of
others have been, and these mysterious irrelevancies lead
nowhere.*

It went on for many pages, a fairly typical journal for a college kid, desperate, yearning, introspective, tedious, fascinated
by meaninglessness. The knapsack was there, a Jack's Auto
Repair T-shirt, jeans, white socks from back when I wore those.
The car seemed well cared for. Lenny had walked away as I read
the journal. I walked away to look for her and as I did, I woke
up. Betty stood in the doorway, holding a glass of orange juice.
"It's nine o'clock in the morning," she said. "I was worried about
you. You were talking in your sleep."

"You're back," I said.

"You're looking at me," she said.

She is, as I've mentioned, a psychologist and knows too
much already and so I did not tell her about the dream though
she asked me about it twice. I asked about Lenny and she said
Lenny had left yesterday for Colorado to become a painter.

Had she heard of a hospital called Broadmoor? Yes, of
course, she said. It was a charismatic institution that believed
in insanity as a sacred calling—"all true saints are insane in the
eyes of the world." The place burned down long ago. "How did
you hear about it?' she said.

I had almost been institutionalized in my dream, and if I
had been, where would I have awakened—at Broadmoor or in
her guest bedroom? I had left the car in the woods, never to be

seen again, and left behind the young man who wrote "There is no way out"—there is a way out, of course, and I awoke in a world that felt greener that morning. A mysterious mist rose out of the grass in Betty's yard, and in her backyard pond water lilies bloomed and bullfrogs chuckled to themselves. When you realize that this badly designed amphibian is allowed the bliss of courtship and copulation, it restores your faith in divine mercy. Lightning bugs are flashing their salacious messages, cicadas are humming and the bumblebees, who according to our best engineers, are not able to fly—their wings are too short—are flying around anyway. The benefit of a short life expectancy is a lack of self-knowledge that would only weigh you down.

"Darlene came back yesterday," Betty said. "She came back from Willmar, where she'd been working at The Lucky Spud. That's that mashed potato chain that serves the Big Cheesie and the Land O' Gravy. She gained 10 pounds working there and Dorothy begged her to come back and finally she did."

It shook me up, finding my journal from when I was young with all the synthetic despair in it. It struck me that I could've gotten into the Mustang and backed it up and I would've been back in 1969, living my life over again but not knowing what I know now—that would be too exquisitely painful—and I'm glad I didn't do that. So here I am, not a time traveler, just a customer at the counter in the Chatterbox—"How's it going, sweetheart," says Darlene and fills my cup with coffee. I went away from Lake Wobegon for more than 10 years and she still remembers that I take my coffee black, no whole milk, no 2 percent, no cream. This moves me. Everything moves me these days. I'm a pile of feeling, maybe the World's Largest. We weren't brought up to be romantics. We've been to Minneapolis, we've seen what romanticism leads to, it leads to nature photography, people going to the woods and coming back with several hundred pictures they're anxious to show you, or it leads to prose poems about life as a journey, which it isn't. We live ours right here at home. "It's never been better, Darlene darling," I said. "What can I get for you, honey?" she said. I said, "Just let me gaze on your beauty for two minutes and I won't need anything else." She said, "You're the second man to tell me that today."

His name was Newman. And she poured him coffee and said, "How's your day going, sweetheart?" and suddenly his day was going better. Nobody had called him sweetheart in recent memory, because he was a trucker and lived in his sleeper cab and had given up on romance years ago. He'd come to town as an advance man for Dick Dixon, to check out the progress of the Keep On Truckin' project, and he arrived just as the project had crashed. Hilmar Bakken and the Hoerschgens walked away with bushels of cash, but Mr. Dixon had suffered badly after his cheese attack and the federal government was on his back and his wife ran away with his accountant and her lawyers were dismantling him piece by piece and he was said to be living in a motel in Daytona and doing a podcast, *This Could Happen to You*. He was up the creek and so was the trucker, Mr. Newman.

He told Darlene he was heading home to North Carolina, but then he didn't. He fixed her dinner one evening, on a grill in the woods where his truck was parked. He got his banjo out of the cab and sang to her, soulful ballads about tragic occurrences. As it turned out, she didn't mind the banjo at all. Its plinkiness made her think of raindrops. She invited him over for dinner two days later. It was pork ribs, which he didn't mind. They talked for three hours. The next night, he confessed that he loved her, helplessly and unreasonably, and once that bridge was crossed, they crossed a couple more bridges in about 15 minutes—surf pounded on the shore, herons flew up from the lake, wild horses galloped across the meadow, a saxophone played.

A week later, she told people, "I am thinking of buying the cafe from Dorothy and getting me a liquor license. Then I'd stay open for the dinner hour. Serve wine. This town needs a good restaurant. I saw a nice cafe in Oshkosh, Wisconsin, last week. Thatcher's. Good menu, steak but also big salads and paella and shrimp gumbo. And a big wine cellar."

Oshkosh? How did she slip away to Oshkosh without us knowing it? This is a small town. We know where everybody is. She had gone to Oshkosh without telling us. "How long were you there?" Two days and two nights. "Who'd you go with?" A friend. "Oh. A friend. Someone from around here?" Depends on what you mean by 'around here.' "Oh. That must've been fun." It was, she said.

The friend, obviously, was Mr. Newman, and in his ecstasy and idiocy, he told her he was going to give up cigars and lose 50 pounds and then he hoped to marry her. She said no, she liked his cigars. She loved him having flesh she could get a grip on and hang onto. He said, "I am not worthy of you and I am going away until I make myself worthy." He'd been raised strict Baptist so there was no arguing with his self-abasement—he left a note under the cafe door one night saying she had changed his life and given him hope and now he must become a man worthy of her love and he took off in his truck and headed west, careening

from town to town, feeling lost without her, chain-smoking sto-
gies, drinking Jim Beam, listening to songs in which the girl dies
in the third verse and the lover looks for a cliff to throw himself
off. He went on a bender in Butte, Montana, got sky-high and
sat in a park singing "Lovesick Blues," which people who loved
that song did not approve of it being played on the banjo. They
called the cops, and he took a swing at a deputy and landed in
the hoosegow, where he shared a cell with two bad eggs named
Izzy and Dizzy, who were in for destruction of property. They
had stomped on flower beds and torn down white picket fences
and ripped off blue shutters. Only blue, not green or yellow or
white. Senseless violence. Mr. Newman sat in the cell for nine
days, eating baloney sandwiches and drinking Kool-Aid, and
thinking about Darlene, and he was *six days away* from release
when his idiot roommates pulled out a smuggled zip gun and
grabbed him for a shield and busted out through the back door,
stole a squad car, sped north on gravel roads at 2 a.m., trailed by
flashing blue lights and a chopper overhead, blew past a roadblock at the Canadian border, and raced over a plowed field at
100 mph, Mr. Newman in the back seat, bouncing off the ceiling, crashing through a farmyard, sideswiping a chicken coop,
hitting a propane tank, which burst into flames, which stopped
them finally. Like so many desperadoes on the run, they were
not wearing seat belts. All three were badly banged up, he especially. He returned to Minnesota after weeks in the hospital,
having sold his semi to pay the bill for reconstructive surgery on
his face, and he called Darlene from a truck stop in East Grand
Forks, and her mother answered and said, "She's out with Bob,"
and that sent him into agonies of jealousy, which caused him to

193

lose 47 pounds in three weeks, sitting in an abandoned shed and not eating, and finally he sent her a Hallmark get well card on which he wrote, "I've learned my lesson," he said. "I am who I am, and you are the love of my life." And came to see her. And found that Bob was her cousin. And they married in a fever the next day. They walked into church and she stopped in the vestibule and said, "I forgot to ask. Are you married?" "Now?" he said. She nodded. "No," he said. And that was good enough for her. The wedding supper was pork roast and mashed potatoes and banana cream pie, in the corner booth of the Chatterbox with Clint and Irene, who had stood up for them, and after all Mr. Newman had been through, yes, he was very happy, you might even say delighted.

19

FITZGERALD

I was losing track of time, being away from my big city life. "Is it May or June?" I asked Betty.

"June," she said. "Late June."

"It feels like August. I've lost all sense of time. I feel like my mother's going to walk in and say, 'I've been looking all over for you. We're supposed to be at gospel meeting in half an hour, get a clean shirt on.'"

"It happens in June, around the solstice. Agelessness. I read a book about it."

"I feel lost and adrift. Have you been feeding me cheese?"

"Never. What happened to Hilmar Bakken?" she said.

He killed his dogs and took the money and bought a little condo in Seattle. He thought he was dying, and he didn't want to die in Minnesota where people'd feel sorry for him and when he got to Seattle he felt much improved and decided he wanted to go to sea. He went to a doctor for the first time in his life and found out he had prostate trouble, and a surgeon lasered out a chunk of it and they gave him a DNA test and found out he's only about 41 percent Norwegian with some Celt and Anglo and about one-third Spanish and that completely clarified his thinking. He'd *felt* Spanish and now he had an excuse to go all the way. He dyed his hair black and wore it in a slight ponytail and grew a black mustache. He went on cruise after cruise, Caribbean, Mediterranean, Baltic, Atlantic, everywhere but Norway, his spirit lightened, he became a charmer, wore ornamental shirts with silver studs, learned dialogue from romance novels he found around the ship: *I love being at sea, every day like the one before except better. Life is a backward glance, a wave, and then off to what's new. I never knew my father. So I set out to be who I wished he had been.* When asked, he was Rhode Island–born and had made a career in the submarine corps, which nuclear secrecy forbade him to discuss. He enjoyed being courted by mature European widows and spent hours around the piano in the lounge, singing old standards off the teleprompter. He could waltz, jitterbug, and approximate a tango. There are caterpillars who anchor themselves to a stick and create a chrysalis around themselves and two weeks later emerge as butterflies. Hilmar punched out a cow who shat on him and he got a whole new life out of it.

"Speaking of Hilmar, when do we get to read your book?"

"Never. I decided not to finish it. I threw it away. I'm done."

"What's the problem?"

For one thing, the manuscript fell on the floor and the pages (unnumbered) got out of order, and I tried to arrange them and nothing made sense anymore. I worked at it for an hour. I got unhappier and unhappier. This happens to me often. I put my nose to the grindstone and write and rewrite and look at it a week later and it's sloppy, verbose, wordy, long-winded, tedious, monotonous, redundant. And also repetitive. I don't think as fast as other people do, sometimes it takes me hours. I'm still trying to figure out things that happened decades ago. Everyone else has made up their minds but not me.

It had been 30 years since I said on TV, "Not the end of the world but you can see it from there," and I portrayed the town as populated by inarticulate men and crazed bachelor farmers, a stronghold of mediocrity and suspicion, and now I decided to live that down and not be the betrayer of my people. I want to be a loyal son of the Maroon and Gray, our Lake Wobegon. So I dumped my novel, all 200 pages, heavily marked, into Betty's trash barrel, and decided to pack my bags in the morning and leave town quietly and get to work on the memoir.

I'd been working on books for years and what I learned is: *Nothing you do is ever good enough.* This should be inscribed over the doorway to education, not *Founded in the faith that men are ennobled by understanding.* Ha! Humbug! There is no ennoblement going on, only confusement and stupidification. I learned that from Scott Fitzgerald when he lived in a retirement home near Loring Park in Minneapolis, and, no, he didn't collapse of a heart attack in Sheilah Graham's apartment in LA, he went to AA, not LA, and worked for the Billy Graham association as a gardener and was known as Fran and he hated *The Great Gatsby* and refused to allow a copy of it anywhere near him. I remember him saying, "My God. *So we beat on, boats against the current, borne back ceaselessly into the past.* Where did I come up with that nonsense? People will think I'm back on the sauce. *The inexhaustible variety of life?* It sounds like a sophomore at Vassar."

Nobody read his books anymore, for which he was grateful. He loved gardening and canasta and bread baking and croquet, none of which you'll find in his fiction. He and Zelda lived in a two-room apartment and were quite sweet on each other and fiercely private. She changed her name to Agnes. I met them in 1964 when he was 68, and I recognized him and told him that I was a writer too. He said, "Whenever you feel like writing a book, just remember that all the people in this world aren't as interested in your life as you are." He smiled understandingly in a way that seemed to understand me as I understood myself, and believe as I believed, that I was no better than average and probably somewhat less. I promised him that I'd never divulge his secret and I've kept that promise until now. He hated to hear that the University was offering courses in creative writing. He said, "Writers should be discouraged, not the other way around. Very few people have anything worthwhile to say—I can think of only three or four—and that leaves a hundred thousand who were meant to be raising tomatoes or sweeping sidewalks. A well-kept sidewalk is worth more in the greater scheme of things than an inferior novel. One good farmer is worth the whole damn bunch of lousy novelists put together. They're careless and they smash up things and let other people clean up the mess they made. That's why Ernest put the shotgun in his mouth. He saw that he was going to live too long and likely write again and it would be a mess, and he didn't want people to forget he'd been great at one time. That would be his final defeat and he decided not to go there. You can't live forever, but if you write a great book, full of the mystery and beauty of the world, you can imagine you might. I wanted *Gatsby* to be my great book, my green light, a book that would write itself, inspired by romantic readiness and the gift of hope, but it kept receding, eluding me, though I ran faster and faster, arms outstretched, and then I wrote that godawful line about 'boats against the current' and it was three o'clock in the morning and I had lived too long with a single dream, swimming underwater and holding my breath, and I sobered right up and made plans to return to Minnesota. And here I have held two opposed ideas in my mind at the same time—I am a great man and I am a groundskeeper—and I retain the ability to function. I mow the lawn and the world is better for it. Advertising contributes nothing and journalism contributes very little; a well-mowed lawn is worth slightly more than a newspaper, and 'slightly' is good enough for me." He was raking grass clippings in the yard of the Graham Evangelistic Association as he said this, and a man in a suit came out and said, "Francis, when you're finished here, could you come in and help in the cafeteria?" and Fitzgerald smiled at him, a smile that spoke of diamonds and moonlight and champagne, and headed for the food line to dish up macaroni. He seemed quite satisfied doing that, saying hello to the employees and ladling the hotdish and green beans, asking, "Would you like rye bread or whole wheat?" as if they were two different roads in life.

I'd run into him when I was reading *Tender Is the Night* my last year in high school. My mother saw the book and said, "I know a Fran Fitzgerald, he's a friend of your Aunt Ina's, he works for Billy Graham." I scoffed, of course. I knew that Fitzgerald had died in 1940. But she insisted I look him up, and that summer I got a job as a dishwasher at the Evangeline Hotel by Loring Park and I walked over to the address Ina gave me and there he was, an old man with white hair slicked back but he had an elegant bearing that suggested an interesting backstory. I showed him the book and he said, "What about it? How'd you find me?" But when he found out I was a dishwasher, not a literature professor, he relaxed. "That was from a restless time," he said. "A haunted lonely time, poignant in a way, even enchanting, but in the end, shamelessly wasteful and selfish. I loved Paris, I loved New York, but it occurred to me once—I was in a little cafe in Montmartre and I heard a woman singing to her French lover, a song I knew from childhood—*Minnesota, hail to thee, hail to thee our state so dear, thy light shall ever be a beacon bright and clear*—she sang it in French, *Votre lumière sera toujours un phare lumineux et clair*—and she put her arms around him. '*France ou moi?*' I heard the whole thing. The air was thick with moonlight and mystery, but she knew where she belonged and needed to be there. 'I am a Golden Gopher,' she said. Except there is no French word for gopher so she said she was a golden squirrel: *Je suis un écureuil.* Which made him laugh. Which offended her. The most precious thing is to know from whom you have sprung and be true to your school. To be read and admired by strangers is no great feat, what is remarkable is enduring friendship. He laughed at Minnesota, and she stubbed out her cigarette and spat on the ground and that was that. It is what it is. *C'est ce que c'est.*"

The memory of Fitzgerald was a great revelation, and I realized that my book, *The Lake Wobegon Virus*, wasn't worth the trouble it would cause. I thought, "I'm retired. Out of the game. My life is a story of misdirection. Forty years ago, my wife sent me to the store for plastic wrap, and the store was out and I asked a man where I could buy Cling and he said, "My name is Kling" and he was a radio manager and that's how I got into radio. I needed a sponsor and Jack of Jack's Auto Repair in my hometown offered to do it because he was hopelessly in love with my cousin. He courted her by sending her a tape of his favorite song, "I Got It Bad and That Ain't Good," and she hated it and married a tire dealer and broke his heart. I kept going with radio because I had no other possibilities. I wasted half my life on it and now I'm trying to live longer so it'll be less than half. I'm in favor of mandatory retirement at 40. Gives a man a chance for a decent second act.

Betty begged me to let her read the book and I said no. I said, "It was going along pretty well and then I came to a part where God speaks to a man through his dog, Fred, and it's the simple factual truth and nobody will accept it, so why bother?"

"Let me see it," she said.

"I threw it away. Too late. Don't give it another thought."

20

BACK TO MINNEAPOLIS

I packed my bag, fending off Betty's questions, and drove downtown and parked behind the Chatterbox and went in the back door to pick up a caramel roll and an apple for the drive back to Minneapolis.

Dorothy said, "They're small, sweetheart. You want two?" These are rolls the size of softballs with about 10 times the minimum daily adult requirement of caramel, but as long as she had opened the door to a second caramel roll, I considered the option. It's a long drive to Minneapolis. The sugar would keep me alert. A number of Wobegonians have been killed in traffic accidents on that highway, most of them on the way home, but still. It would be a shame to lie bleeding in the twisted wreckage of my car in the ditch under a semi loaded with lumber and think about the caramel roll I didn't have. "How about some coffee with that, darling?" she said. As a matter of highway safety, I thought, a coffee would be an excellent idea.

"You don't want that to go, do you? You might hit a bump and spill on yourself. Stick around. What's your rush?" she said.

Well, that was a whole other question, so I sat down to think about it and she poured me a mug of coffee, black. People who take milk with their coffee are trying to mitigate the purpose of coffee, which is to awaken the conscience. They are tea-drinkers at heart who imagine tea will lead to writing haiku and unfortunately it does.

> *I write these short lines*
> *With fear in my heart that they*
> *Will make a haiku.*

What the world needs is not poetic whispers but the workings of conscience. I came home to work on a pointless project involving sainthood, but I did confront my faithless and hopeless youth and I declined institutionalization and in the process I had seen my friends and family lose their inhibitions, if only briefly, and speak freely and the town survived it all. I sipped my coffee and it stung the roof of my mouth and I was grateful for that.

"So how's it going for you today?" Dorothy said. It's not a simple question at nine o'clock in the morning. Usually, I wake up feeling ambitious, but this morning I had wanted to stay in bed and sleep some more but had shamed myself to arise and shower and put on a suit and tie by thinking grievous thoughts of unpublished poets, pitchers whose arms went bad, football stars who got dinged too often, standup comics who didn't keep up with the times, child geniuses whose genius is useless. E.g., the boy in St. Paul who knew by heart the names of every performer on *A Prairie Home Companion* and which of the 750 shows they had performed on, which is astonishing for about 10 minutes, but is pointless given the existence of Google and so today, at 28, he works in a soup kitchen ladling out tuna casserole to other unfortunates. The world is full of them. So what right do I have to lie abed?

"I'm okay," I said. And I seemed to be. I felt good about throwing my novel into the trash. For many years, when I've had a hard day and can't get to sleep at night, I imagine walking out of my apartment house and finding 20 reporters on the sidewalk, camera crews, men and women with notebooks, and they want to know how I feel about having been given the Nobel Prize in Literature, and by the time I thank the Swedish Academy for this honor, I am asleep.

Sometimes for variety's sake, I'm at the White House and Bill Clinton is pinning the National Arts Medal on me. These fantasies are bread and butter but like all fantasies, they lose their usefulness and go dim, and now, sitting in the Chatterbox, I realized I have washed ashore in the same town where I launched forth years ago. I've come full circle and am a nobody again, thank God, the beautiful symmetry of life.

A street-cleaning truck came by and vacuumed the gutters and scrubbed the pavement and the driver waved to me. It was Marlon. As I drank my coffee, I turned and there was Alice. I braced myself for the attack. "I'm glad I get to see you before you leave town, I want to thank you," she said. Dorothy handed her a menu and she ordered steak and eggs with hash browns and onions. Myrtle and Florian came in, she in her jet-black wig and purple pantsuit, he in coveralls and Powdermilk cap. She was muttering at him about why in God's name did he forget his hearing aids at home and he looked contented as usual. They've been at odds for 50 years and that's how they maintain their balance. She wanted to sell the farm and move into a senior high-rise in St. Cloud and Florian resisted selling the farm by going to estate sales and purchasing junk machinery, ancient mowers, windrowers, wood chippers, log splitters, headers, feeders, manure spreaders, mulchers, cultivators, sprayers, harvesters, discs and harrows, bunchers, balers, scrapers, augers, loaders, tractors, tillers, plows, scythes, skidders, sawmills, combines, grinders, graders, planters, processors, forwarders, sealers—40 acres of useless machinery where the weeds grow tall around the junk, and the farm is unsaleable and if you ask Florian what he keeps it for, he says, "Waiting for a good offer. Most of this stuff, they don't make it anymore. Can't buy it anywhere. If they want it, they have to come to me."

Then, this summer, he said yes, he'd have the junk hauled away so they could move to the condo. This threw Myrtle for a loop but she'd been begging him for years and didn't know how to unbeg. He met a trucker in the Sidetrack Tap who said he'd come haul the junk away but then he took off for Montana and sold the truck so Florian is still waiting. Meanwhile he's bought a few more machines. Young men grew old fast working those machines and died young bringing in the crops and tending the land, and did it bring them pleasure or enlightenment? In his opinion, no. So he devoted himself to a life of contemplation. And so shall I.

I felt a hand on my shoulder. It was Clint. "Saw your suitcase in your car. You leaving us?" he said.

Dorothy brought me the two caramel rolls and I sliced them

into small pieces so I could offer them to the others, knowing they'd decline, and I'd get to eat all of it, but instead they said, "Thanks" and ate two apiece. Dorothy came over and sat down with a cup of coffee.

Clint said, "I'd like two slices of toast and a coffee with milk."

She said, "Get it yourself. I'm on break." So he went and put bread in the toaster and poured a cup of coffee. "Where do you keep the milk?" he said.

"Look around," she said. "If you can't find it, the cat has some in a dish on the floor." She looked at me. "What did you write about me? Did you have a tall angular man with wavy reddish hair walk in and ask for breakfast in a foreign accent and fall in love with my eggs and sausage and take me away in his private jet to his mansion in Monterey?"

"No," I said, "I'm afraid it lacks plausibility."

"I'm going to pretend you didn't say that," she said.

Alice and Clint and Dorothy and I sat around the table, and 10 feet away, Myrtle told Florian that she had seen a perfect apartment in St. Cloud, two bedrooms, a laundry, and a balcony looking out at the Mississippi River. The previous tenants had died in a murder-suicide so it was available furnished, linens, towels, dishware, everything, and cable paid for through the end of the year.

Pastor Liz walked in and saw us and pulled up a chair. "Mind if a theologian joins you?" she said.

"Okay by me," said Alice, "but let's start out in a spirit of forgiveness."

"Fine," said Liz and we all said it together: *Forgive us our sins as we forgive those who sin against us and lead us not into temptation but deliver us from evil.* Liz said that Senator K. was feeling very ill this morning, and Mary called and told her he doesn't want pastoral care, he is afraid of healing, he wants to take his leave. She turned to me: "Someday you'll be the oldest living survivor, and people will be avoiding you on the street for fear you'll tell them one of your stories that they've already heard a hundred times."

I said, "No, I'm done. I've told enough stories. I was meant to be a bus driver or a short-order cook but I wandered into the storytelling field in order to make myself appear intelligent and instead of fulfilling a useful function I became a mere decoration. Name me one great writer who was happy. Name one. Other than Solomon. For a writer, the secret of happiness is to read *Don Quixote* and recognize that Cervantes is 10 times the writer you'll ever be and don't bother wasting time in the attempt. Do something useful with your life, like run a day-care center. From now on, when I get up from this table, I intend to stay strictly within the bounds of truth. Though I will say, in my own defense, that I have done some good with fiction."

"Are you about to tell the story about giving Bert's eulogy?" said Alice. "I've heard it, I don't need to hear it again."

"No, this is a different eulogy, one for my classmate Rich. He went to California to visit an uncle and he rented a car and was driving to Santa Barbara and enjoying the scenery when he came over a hill where moments before the tailgate of a semitruck had sprung open and the road was all yellow with bananas and he slammed on his brakes, the worst thing to do when driving on bananas, and he skidded 200 feet and into a eucalyptus tree, and died with the smell of cough drops in his nose. His wife knew, and so did her sisters and Rich's brother, that there was no uncle involved and he'd gone to spend a weekend with a former student, Emily, whom he was (as it turned out) fatally attracted to. I gave a eulogy, and it was my job to create an uncle and spare the family the shame. I created a great uncle, a veteran of D-Day, a patriot and poet and potato farmer who quoted Emerson, an *Aristotle Contemplating the Bust of Homer* of uncles, brave, sensitive, down to earth, and dying of tuberculosis contracted in a Nazi prison camp. And I took out the bananas and substituted three small children crossing the road and Rich swerved to avoid them. Even Rich's wife who knew the truth about the bastard was moved to tears. He was a jerk but, thanks to me, he was forgiven."

The story of Rich led to Liz's story of the Lutheran pastors on a pontoon boat and Clint's story of a tomato-sucking dog and Dorothy told about Bruno the fishing dog and Clint told about his dad's encounter with the black Lab who came up out of the hole in the ice and caused Oscar to lose his English, and by then it was noon, and Mary had come to report that Senator K. was feeling a good deal better. Dorothy said, "If you're going to the Cities, you better get going. Unless you'd like lunch." She brought out a pan of macaroni and cheese hot from the oven. "Pasteurized, don't worry," she said. "You turn your head and the cheese goes past your eyes." A joke from third grade. It smelled good. We noted the generous amount of peas in it, a Dorothy innovation.

"Byron loved peas in everything. He loved peas in spaghetti," Mary said. "That's how he died. I was making spaghetti for lunch and he went down the basement to get a package of frozen peas, and on his way back up he sat down on the steps. Next-to-last step from the top. I was on the phone with my sister and I asked him if he was okay and he said, 'I'm fine' and when I opened the door to the stairs, he was gone. His eyes were open and he was dead. I called the rescue squad and they came and worked on him but he had no pulse. I sat down beside him and put my arm around him and told him I loved him and always would love him. And I took the frozen peas from his hand and put them in the refrigerator." Clarence walked in the cafe, and he could tell from how quiet we were that Mary was talking about a death, so he waited for her to finish. She said Byron had seen a doctor a month before and everything was fine. "So I called up the kids, John in Boston and Ronnie in Texas and Judy and Diana in Tucson, and Bill, and Mr. Lundberg and his son came and took the body away and I took a nap and cleaned up, and by six or so, the kids were all there and we were hugging and Diana was pretty torn up but we were okay. They wanted to hear how it happened so I told them and I asked if they wanted some spaghetti for supper—I'd made it already, and I brought it to the table and we said grace and they served themselves and then Diana looked at it and she said, 'Are these the peas Daddy brought up from the basement when he died?' I said yes. She said, 'You are serving us the Death Peas?' She couldn't get over it. We were eating the peas Daddy held in his hand as he died. I don't think she's forgiven me to this day. John pointed out that Byron had touched everything in this house including the chair she was sitting in, and she said, 'Yes, but we're not eating it.' Oh my. What a day. That was five years ago. Death peas."

As she told about Byron's death, we could hear the marching band in the distance and then it came booming by, a drum
major in a grenadier hat and white jacket and pants, clarinets in
the front row, trumpets and trombones, a line of drummers in
the rear. Today was the Fourth of July. In all the drama of the
cheese and the lost Mustang and the discarded novel, I'd forgotten all about it.

It was truly inspiring. The military bearing of adolescents
in uniform, their posture, the high-stepping march, the serious faces, the sheer focus. Dickie the drum major thrusting his
scepter high over his head to the rattle of the snare drums—the
boom of the bass drum and the oomph of the tubas—the dinging of the xylophone, the sheer pride of it all—it was everything
the old Knutes parading on the 17th of May were not—they
were the dying past and this was the eager future—but where
did our children learn this? We are a modest rural community
of ordinary people, we are not a Prussian elite officer corps seeking world domination, so what is the high-stepping to drum
cadence all about? It is about youthful idealism, and good God
do we need it. It's not about domination but about pride, a necessary fuel whether you are picking potatoes or repairing transmissions or writing a novel.

The band slammed their right feet down and came to a stop,
the drums still keeping time, and Dickie turned, back arched, and
aimed himself a quarter-turn and counted to four and headed
up McKinley Street, and the band wheeled smartly behind him
and all of us in the cafe were stunned with admiration. "End of
the world"? No way. The world has just begun to begin.

211

21

CORN

It was a dazzling Fourth even without Uncle Sam on stilts and the circus bandwagon with sunburst wheels and carvings of elephants and wizards on the sides and the 16-Percheron hitch, the teamsters in silk cracking their big whips. No Betsy Ross blanket toss—men in powdered wigs holding a canvas net and throwing a woman wrapped in Old Glory 30 feet in the air— no Whistler's Mothers in gray skirts and capes, marching along and whistling "Colonel Bogey March" and no FFA Precision Pitchfork Drill Team, but it was dazzling nonetheless. The old parade used to go around twice so people who watched it the first time around could march in the second circuit. No time for that now. The old parade died in 2016 when it attracted a crowd of 20,000 and afterward people complained that Clint was too bossy and didn't listen to other people's ideas and so, modest man that he is, he stepped down as chairman of the Fourth and the people with their own ideas came in, sort of, and formed committees and appointed chairpersons, and there was a great deal of discussion, and the next year it was mostly a parade of schoolchildren and was not widely advertised and 2,000 came and now it's just us, which is fine. The old glories fade quickly, time is relentless, our day is brief and when it's done it is so utterly done. We leave behind no legacy, just some papers in a box that somebody else has to throw away. So make the most of the summer.

"Do they still do the Living Flag at the football field?" I said to Alice.

She said yes but it was a smaller Living Flag than it used to be.

I stood up. "Let's go," I said.

She said, "Before we go, I have to apologize for what I said to you. I read your book last night and I'm glad you wrote it. It's mostly true and it has a lot to say, and I was moved by what you wrote about yourself and I'm sorry I misjudged you."

"*The Lake Wobegon Virus*???? How did you get your hands on that?"

"It was in a wastebasket. The pages were out of order but I got it figured out." And she handed it to me. "It's all true except for Lenny—she's not a bacteriologist, she's an epidemiologist."

"Then I guess I'm an apologist. My specialty is regret."

"Oh, enough with the humility," she said.

The five of us fell in behind the band. She gave me the manuscript in a green manila envelope, and the crash and boom of the percussion ahead of us got to me. I wasn't in marching band in school. I was too cool for that. But I don't care about cool anymore. I want to tell about the people I left behind when I set out to become successful, now that I'm old and the great democracy of death approaches and success means practically nothing. A few hundred townspeople stood on the field holding red and white and blue umbrellas. Someone gave me a white one and I stood in a row of whites, between two rows of reds, forming stripes of Old Glory. Alice was on one side of me, an old man on the other. We crowded in tight, umbrellas over our heads, forming a flag that we ourselves could not see, but we could feel our own solidarity. It was very moving. To me, it was. Having set out at a young age to distinguish myself as a unique individual, and here I was, anonymous, in service of an ideal. The band struck up "America" and we sang, "My country 'tis of thee," and then the school fight song and then a boy read into a microphone, "Breathes there the man with soul so dead who never to himself hath said, 'This is my own, my native land,'" and then, to my amazement, a girls' trio sang:

Wobegon, I remember oh so well how peacefully among the woods and fields you lie. My Wobegon, I close my eyes and I can see you just as clearly as in days gone by.

My song. I wrote that. And the verse about *My old dog takes his walk, sniffing ev'ry tree. Ev'ry smell seems to tell his biography.* And *By the barn, cattle turn, murmur in the pen. Strong and pure, cow manure: I know where I am. I am home again.* And *Little town, I love the sound of water sprinklers on the land. The siren tune at 12 o'clock noon, the booming of the marching band.*

I told Alice, "That's my song. They're singing my song."

She said, "I have no idea what you're talking about." The old man said, "I remember that song from when I was a kid."

It was a miracle. A song I wrote long ago had now become

215

Anonymous. A great tribute, to become part of the common language. I wrote it to show off my talent, and now it was public property.

We stood and listened to a teacher read the first paragraphs of the Declaration ("We hold these truths to be self-evident, that all men are created equal...") and we sang the National Anthem, the sopranos floating up high over "the land of the free," and then the band marched off with a great ruffle and flourish, and we turned in our umbrellas. Alice said it was the biggest Living Flag in several years. She'd been worried about the number of e-mails she'd gotten from people saying, yes, they'd take part but not if they had to stand next to so-and-so. A measure of peace had been restored. Father Wilmer was in the Flag next to Father Powers, Liz was there with some Lutheran ladies, and Hilmar Bakken had flown in from Seattle to be on hand. He looked very snazzy in a blue suit with red tie and white shirt.

The crowd smelled sweet corn and that lit a fire under us and we headed for the Our Lady parking lot, where a dozen Knights of Columbus were husking at high speed, grabbing ears from a trailer full of bushel baskets, and ladies tended the pots of boiling water on the line of camp stoves. I bought six tickets for a buck apiece from Ingrid at the cash table and she said, "Hang on to those, they're for the big drawing too" and I got three ears of corn and slathered them in butter and salted them down and stood in the crowd of eaters, and bit in. It was transformational. I am just a sentimental old man but the taste of fresh hot corn filled me with love of my town and my country. People had worked hard to pick the corn rapidly at the last minute so that it traveled from field to pot to your hand in 20 minutes, which is the difference between very nice corn and transcendent corn.

Alice said the feast and the lottery were financed by Rollie Hochstetter, whose granddaughter Natalie had that spring earned a bundle online at the age of eight after she visited her grandparents and a month later they noticed an odd item on the Visa bill for $12,345.67, which she'd put into stocks, looking at the listings and seeing shapes of animals and where the animal's left hind foot was placed, that's where she put the money, which now was worth almost $64,000 and a month later had grown to $117,000. They tried to get her to do more but she had lost interest. Rollie cashed in the stocks and put half of it into a scholarship fund for little Natalie and donated the other half to the Fourth of July, so that's what paid for the corn and the convertible for the lottery was donated by Clarence. A 1958 Ford. Clint drew the winning ticket and played it for drama, reading off the numbers slowly and came to the last digit and noticed Mary was in agony, shaking her head, *No no no,* so he said, "Excuse me," and revised the next-to-last number to her vast relief. She was worried that Senator K. would own a white convertible and be a menace to the town and exterminate several kids on bikes. It was won by a nun from St. Cloud, Sister Frances, who'd forgotten she'd bought a ticket. She'd renounced material wealth and now she'd won some. On a sudden impulse, she gave the ticket to Father Wilmer, not knowing he'd been defrocked, and he was thrilled. He'd made a date with a clergywoman named Patricia in Fargo and now he had a car that would compare well to other cars in Fargo.

It was my first sweet corn of the year. I was standing between the Krebsbachs, Carl and Margie, and Lena was there with her dog, Bruno, who once was a fishing dog but lost interest after he was bitten by a bullhead and now was eating an ear of corn that hung from his neck. Clarence was chewing on an ear, working his vertically, circling the ear, and I was working mine horizontally—like a typewriter—and our eyes met in a glance of brotherhood, and I was moved to stand up and give a speech. Nobody asked me to. I stood up on an empty wheelbarrow and Clint dinged on a glass and there was silence, except for quiet mastication.

I am an old man, privileged to return to the place of my birth, and I am only sorry to see so few of my generation with us today—they went off like Cortés and Pizarro in search of conquest and adventure, and instead they found jobs in offices and spouses who don't understand them, and now they're old and disillusioned, stranded in Florida and Arizona in luxurious death camps, trapped by clement weather. You and I who stayed where God planted us are the fortunate ones. We had all the advantages of a bitter winter. Every year, nature made several sincere attempts to kill us. But there always was someplace colder. Ely, Minnesota, on the Canadian border. If it was 10 below here, it was 17 below in Ely, so you got a sense of God's mercy. You lay in bed and read a story about San Diego in the National Geographic *and thought how wonderful it would be to live there and play golf in January. Every year, you reexamined your life. People in California don't have that opportunity. The weather is always pleasant and if you can't be happy in Southern California, there's no hope for you, whereas in Minnesota we live on hope. We sit in our cave, the wind howling in the chimney and we think, I could go to La Jolla and be 27 years old. People in La Jolla can't go to Minnesota; they would walk out of the airport and freeze to death before they get to the rental car lot. But a Minnesotan has options.*

And then winter is over, and we have a cold rainy spring, and then it is summer, and now we know why we stayed. There are four main pleasures in life, the pleasure of knowledge, and the pleasure of walking with God, and the pleasure that some of you thought of first, and then there is sweet corn, fresh from the field, quickly husked, briefly boiled, buttered and salted, and here we are, drunk on it, out of our minds with happiness. I don't look happy because I have a fundamentalist face, but sweet corn is taken internally, not applied to the face, and inside I am a completely happy man. It's my belief that no person can have all four pleasures, and if I had to choose which to sacrifice, I would give up knowledge, which as anyone can tell you only leads to misery because with increased knowledge comes the knowledge that many people know much more than you and they are assholes. Absolute nincompoops have no idea of their nincompoopery, but the scholar climbing toward the summit sees others ahead of him and they are rolling boulders down the slope, trying to kill him.

No, sweet corn is the summum bonum, the sine qua non, due to its rarity—a pleasure denied to most of the earth, but God is generous to the Midwest to make up for our miserable climate, our blazing summer with tornadoes and bleak fall and deadly winter and rainy spring, with a few pleasant days ruined by mosquitoes the size of hummingbirds, mosquitoes that go deep, searching for arteries, insect repellent has no effect on them, a crucifix helps but you have to hit them very hard. What we are enjoying right now, you and I, is a pleasure available to a chosen few—you won't find it in Paris or London or Rome, it was grown right here by people you and I ran around with on the playground, our cousins, our old pals, back in the day of the big garden in the backyard, back when our aunts brought us up in the basic catechism—Be Kind To Others—Do Not Use The Lord's Name In Vain—Honor Your Mother and Father—and Always Give Thanks for Life's Good Things, and so I will simply add this: I love you all more and more, and forgive me for not saying it long ago but there is nowhere else I would rather be than here with you. God bless you, each and every one.

And I decided to sing. It just seemed like the right thing to do.

O sweet corn, O sweet corn, O sweet corn I can eat.
We're black and white and Asian and we are all one nation
and this is an occasion to be
sweet.

I was dancing on a wheelbarrow and I am not a dancer but there I was and others started dancing too. A corn dance.

O freedom, O freedom, O freedom, we are born
To love one another, sister and brother, and put salt and but-
ter on the corn.

It was a slow soulful dance, me coming from arrhythmic people as I do, and then a couple drums felt the urge, a bass and a snare, and we got something going.

O mama, O mama, O mama, look at me.
It's the Fourth of July, and I am feeling high, and this song
will never die, nor will we.

The Lutherans had been waiting to dance until they saw Pastor Liz and Clarence and Arlene dance and there they were, hands up over their heads, so the others did likewise.

O pleasure, O pleasure, some pleasure every day.
Live it cheerfully with grace and charity in the land of the
free, the USA.

There was more but that's enough. I stood down from the wheelbarrow. There was no applause because it wasn't a performance, it was for real. I heard a few soft *Amens*. A couple hundred people watched me deliver this crazed rhapsody with gyrations, and Irene took a video, in which I am eating as I dance, some butter dripping down my chin. I look demented. I am holding a cracker spread with cheese. At one point, I reach back as if to adjust my pants and then decide not to.

Clint walked up, wearing an orange cowboy shirt so bright it would stop traffic. "That was a good speech and not a bad dance. People should confess happiness more often," he said. "I have a friend I met out in that field of wildflowers, back when we drove Dick Dixon out of town. You're a blessed man as I am, and it's good to feel our blessedness and be grateful for it and proclaim it. And also it makes the Lutherans nervous that they're scheduled to speak next."

I told him that I said what I said from the heart, but I am a writer and want the truth and the truth is complicated. We had a good preacher in my childhood who preached on the street with a microphone and a speaker on the roof of his car powered by the car's battery. He gave a great sermon once at Lake Nokomis about Jesus calming the waters of the Sea of Galilee that day when the apostles were scared silly because a crazy man had come shrieking out of a cemetery and Jesus had cast a demon out of him, a naked man waving his arms and screaming—the sort of thing that can ruin your whole day—and then the apostles got in the boat and a storm arose and the apostles were thinking, this guy isn't the Messiah, this guy is bad luck. And then he woke and he stilled the waters. I was standing nearby when the preacher was preaching, and he got so carried away he dropped his Bible on the ground and bent down to pick it up and a blast came out of him like the trombone at the circus, three long notes and a short and a smell strong enough to strip bark off trees, and the preacher did not acknowledge what

222

happened, didn't say, "Oh my heavens" or "Goodness, that was a stinker," he went on as if nothing happened, wanting to maintain his authority, but if you deny your own fart then you've lost your authority and embraced lunacy as an article of faith. So I gave up on authority at that point and I don't trust people at microphones. That's my new philosophy. I became an author so I could show off my superior sensibility, and I'm too old for that now. Nuts to sensibility.

I'd had six ears of fresh sweet corn, buttered, and after six, the effect wears off, so I dropped a couple twenties in the pot, Alice handed me my manuscript that I had dropped on the ground when I did my dance. The wind had blown it around a little, so if there are odd confusing passages in the book, that's why. I'm sorry. I marched back to Main Street and got in my car. The pay phone in front of the cafe, which nobody uses anymore and which is out of service, rang, and I ignored it but it kept ringing and finally I picked it up and said, "Hello." It was my wife. She said, "Where are you? I've been calling you for two days, I was about to call the National Guard." I told her my phone's out of power, I haven't used it in months. She was home from her opera tour in Asia. She said, "I need you. I can't sleep without you. I need you to rub my back." "I'm on my way," I said. I wanted to sleep with her when I met her 28 years ago and now it was nice to find out she couldn't sleep without me. An old story: we marry for concupiscence and we stay married for companionship.

I headed south toward Minneapolis and my apartment near Loring Park, where Fitzgerald and I used to take the bus to Nicollet Field to watch the Millers play the Saints. I don't know why people are so drawn to the story of the doomed artist dying young, I prefer the story of the cheerful artist growing old. I was driving past an auto salvage yard, a mile of wrecked cars, and I had a passing thought of tossing the manuscript out the window to rest among the deceased Fords and Chevies but I was not brought up to throw trash out the window, so I didn't. I had the taste of corn and butter and salt in my mouth with a caramel roll yet to come, I still felt the camaraderie of the Fourth of July, and I could still hear the marching band go high-stepping by and the boom and clatter of the beat, and feel the sweet anonymity of the Living Flag and people singing my song who didn't know it was mine. I am a happy man. It's common to get in a crowd of people who agree with you—you march with the United Writers of Light Verse and enjoy feelings of fellowship while chanting protest limericks, and that's satisfying, but to join a crowd of red, white, and blue umbrellas forming Old Glory on a July afternoon, celebrating a union of the bright and benighted, true believers and delivery boys, the over-taxers and the anti-vaxxers, and people whose credos defy description, is to know civic happiness, so love it. Here we are, one nation under God and (at the moment) under the weakest and most childish leader of our entire history, and we are good to go. I am no genius, but I mean well most of the time. Lake Wobegon almost went to pieces from a cheese-borne virus, but it beat back a disastrous mistake because the women are strong, the men are looking good, the children above average. Maybe the time you spent reading this book would've been better spent listening to the Fauré *Requiem*. So go do that. When you hear the "Sanctus," say a prayer for me and the sweet corn crowd. Thank you. Dismissed.